Merlvinia's Wheels

Stan Pinkneey

First published in the United States of America
by Stan Pinkneey 2025

ISBN 978-1-961853-08-9

1. Books 2. Wheels

Number 1

Wait—when did everyone get a girlfriend?

That's the first thing I think when I get on the

bus. Well, actually the *very* first thing is: What the heck

is the kid in the front seat thinking? He's wearing a

puffy metallic silver jacket. Doesn't he realize we live in

Austin, Texas, and it's a thousand degrees out?

But I forget all about the new kid when I see the

rest of the bus. It seems like every seat I walk by has a

couple in it. Some are just sitting close together. Others

are holding hands. And when I'm halfway back I see

Jordan Vargas, actually making out with a girl.

What the?

At the beginning of the summer, no one was

hanging out with girls—everyone was going swimming,

or maybe to football camp (Jordan) or playing little

league baseball (me). Sure, a couple guys had girlfriends

… the ones who'd been going with the same girl since

second grade. But now, everyone's dating someone.

Or almost everyone.

It's the first day of school and I, Chance Allen Peters, am the only seventh grade guy in the world who's girlfriend-less.

To my left, Jordan Vargas and his new girlfriend are still going at it. I totally want to look away, but quick fact-check: Jordan Vargas is my best friend. Jordan Vargas is a football freak. And Jordan Vargas has never shown one (1) speck of interest in dating—the only thing he's ever wanted to cuddle is a tackling dummy.

But now, he's sloshing his lips and tongue all over this girl. It's like she ate a powdered donut and Jordan's trying to clean off every last speck, as fast as possible. One of them actually lets out a slurp. Gross.

Are you supposed to do that when you kiss? And where did he even learn—

"Yo, Chance!"

There's a shot to my arm, like a rocket just exploded into it. Jordan's not making out anymore; he's grinning at me.

Another fact-check: Punching is Jordan's way of saying Hi. Only, he can bench about fifty thousand pounds.

"Dude," Jordan says, nodding at the empty seat across the aisle.

I slide into the seat, rubbing my sore arm. I haven't seen or even talked to Jordan for almost two weeks, since he left for football camp. He left me a message yesterday saying he was back, but he didn't mention a thing about all this. I want to ask about his all-of-sudden girlfriend, but what would I say?

So, um, this is your girlfriend?

So, um, you guys like making out?

So, um, I'm a huge question-asking dork?

The girl with Jordan leans forward. She's wearing a black tank top and I see her face for the first time. She looks vaguely familiar. Then she lowers her head and looks up, both at the same time—it's like she's saying she knows more than I know, and knows she knows more than I know, and knows I know it. I've seen that look before.

No way.

"What's with the staring?" the girl asks.

When I hear her voice, I know for certain. The girl is Zee Mays. Last year, she ranked first in our class (I was second). Last year, her hair was long and frizzy (now it's short and straight). Last year, she wore super-thick glasses (no more). I can actually see her eyes now. They're light brown, like caramel icing.

"Hello," she says, "calling Chance Peters. Speak much?"

"Huh?"

"I *asked*," Zee says, "what you were staring at." She sits up, extracts her arm from Jordan. "You were watching us like a movie. Like you've never seen a kiss before."

"Ha!" I laugh. "Yup, that's *exactly* right!"

This is one of my best skills—saying the opposite of what people expect. It's especially good when coupled with the quick half-laugh. And it works every time— everyone thinks I'm joking, shakes their heads, moves on. I am extremely convincing.

Zee is just sitting there, staring at me. Crap.

All of a sudden I feel warm. Which isn't surprising since it's mid-August and about 230% humidity outside. But the warm I feel is inside.

"Well, yeah," I say. "I mean, I wasn't watching like that, I was just, uh…"

I *have* seen a kiss before, haven't I?

"He was checking my new look," Jordan says, cutting in.

"Yeah," I say, "I was checking *Jordan*, not you."

Nice save, Jordan.

This is one of the things Jordan's good at—helping people out. Like in fifth grade, when I was walking home from school and cut through the field behind St. Phillip's. I ran into two high school guys, hiding in the weeds and smoking. I was pretty sure they were going to beat me up. But then Jordan rode by. We didn't really know each other, but I called out and told him he had a cool bike. (His bike wasn't really all that great—I was just nervous about the two high schoolers.) Jordan skidded to a stop and asked if I wanted a ride. I said "Heck yes," wedged myself onto his handlebars, and he biked me out of there.

We've been friends ever since.

And now, Jordan's just saved me again, making Zee think I was staring at his new look, not at the two of them making out.

Then I notice his new look.

Jordan Vargas, the guy who usually has bits of Wheaties stuck to his shirt, who sometimes forgets to zip his shorts, is wearing jeans. Black, baggy jeans. Along with a layered polo shirt. And crap—he's even wearing a tie, half-tied and hanging all loose and skinny around his neck.

I check my clothes: brown Wal-Mart sneakers (bought by Mom, last year), gray Wal-Mart shorts (same shopping trip), white Longhorns football T (gift Dad sent, for my birthday).   Was I supposed to dress up? Why didn't Jordan say anything about that either? I start to ask about his clothes, but all I manage to say is:

"Cool tie."

"You like? My bro got it for me."

Jordan has an older brother. He plays football at the high school. He's a starter.

"Zee calls it a leash." Jordan tugs sideways at the tie.

"No," she tells him. "*You* keep calling it that. Not me. Get it straight, dinglemouth."

Jordan apologizes, puts an arm around her. They slide close together, giggling about something.

I slide down in my seat. This is not how I planned the first day of school to start. I keep sliding until all I see is the dark green of the seat in front of me. How come I didn't know? I reach out, running my fingers along the smooth seat fabric. It feels like plastic leather. There's a rip near the bottom, a flap of fabric hanging out, a dark hole leading in. For a second, I see myself crawling inside, where I wouldn't have to worry about saying the right thing, wearing the right clothes, dating the right—anyone.

In my backpack, there's a list on light blue paper (my favorite), folded twice: My Main To-Do List. Right now there are twelve things on it, including #1 get football cleats, #2 figure out latest CYOA (*Choose Your Own Adventure*, these awesome old books Dad gave me), and #12 start flossing (in case Mom ever finds it).

I think about taking the list out, but no way I want Jordan or Zee or anyone to see it. So, in my head, I write a new #1: GET A GIRLFRIEND.

Sweat & Savory

In Texas, there are two things you need to know about seventh grade: First, everyone takes Texas History. Second, every guy starts playing football.

Before that, there's no football in school. Last year some guys played Pee Wee league (like Jordan) and some didn't (like me). Don't get me wrong, it's not that I don't like football—I love it, of course—it was just that Mom couldn't afford both little league baseball and Pee Wee league football. I've been playing baseball since second grade, so I chose that. But in seventh grade, all you have to buy for football are cleats. So today— finally—I'll start my football career.

If Dad were here, he'd be a total spaz. He loves loves loves football, even more than Jordan does. Whenever he'd watch a UT game, he'd sit on the couch in his vintage Earl Campbell jersey, burnt orange running shorts, and—not kidding—his cleats from high school. Like if someone got injured, he could jump in his car, drive to the stadium, and be ready to go in the game, right then.

I can only imagine what outfit he'd pick for himself today. And for me? He'd probably want me to wear an entire uniform to school, helmet and all.

Fact-check: In most places, wearing a complete football uniform to school might be a little weird, but Austin is home of the national champion (multiple times) University of Texas Longhorns. Here, football ranks just below oxygen on the life importance scale.

Which explains why, when the bus pulls up to school, Jordan and all the guys head straight to territory that was off-limits before now, the big double-doors down the hall from the grungy P.E. locker room. Inside those double-doors is the place that (according to the school paper) a third of our budget goes to, the place that's practically a gated community, the place guys would give an arm, leg and lung to belong in: The football locker room.

Every guy heads there, that is, but me.

I'll see the locker room in last period, when we actually have football. More important, in football they assign lockers—in class, you get to choose your seat. So, instead of following Jordan and the herd, I go straight to my room for first period Honors English, and—perfect. I'm the only one here.

One thing I've learned: Strategic seat placement is crucial to classroom success.

I scan the room, weigh some pros and cons, try a few desks, and finally settle on the second row, by the door. Second row so I can hear everything but have a buffer. Next to the door so I can see if anything's happening in the hall. I take out my blue To-Do list and cross off #3a: choose first period seat.

A few minutes later everyone starts walking in. Jordan punches my arm (the non-sore one, thankfully), and sits behind me. Zee takes the seat behind him.

"Dude," Jordan says, "the locker room is awesome! Where were you?"

"Oh yeah," I say. "I forgot."

Jordan gives me a "How in all of Texas could you forget *football*?" look, but a second later his face switches to an "Oh, I get it" look.

He shakes his head at me. "You came here early to pick your seat, didn't you?" he asks.

"Maybe."

"And I bet," Jordan continues, "if I look in your

backpack, you'll have one of those little lists, with something like 'pick seat #4' on it, right?" He kicks the back of my chair once, for emphasis.

I try not to smile. "No."

"No?" Jordan grins, reaching for my backpack.

"Okay, okay! There's a list. But, I didn't put the actual seat number on it."

"Dude, you are so weird sometimes."

This feels good. I haven't talked to Jordan in it seems like forever, but now it's getting back to normal. I want to ask him about Zee, his new clothes, and football camp. I know they worked him hard there, since he only called me twice the whole time. But before I can say anything, he's twisted around and leaning way back, twirling a strand of Zee's hair.

I really hope they don't start sugar-slurping in Honors English.

I turn back around, just as the kid from the front of the bus hurries into the room. The bell rings and he takes the front corner seat, right beside the teacher's desk. Does he sit up front for everything? I picture his chair attached to the teacher's desk like a motorcycle sidecar. He's still wearing the silver jacket from the bus—it's got a huge SPACE CAMP CADET patch on the back, and another just below it that says KEVIN.

Who wears something like that to school? Austin, we have a problem.

The class goes quiet as our teacher stands. She looks super young, and super serious. "Good morning. I'm Ms. Fernandez. Welcome to first period, Honors English."

Her glasses have those heavy square rims, the kind that make it hard to tell exactly where she's looking.

"I'd like to start by having each of you tell me a little about yourself."

Ms. Fernandez is dressed up, too. She's wearing a blue-and-white striped shirt tucked into wrinkle-free navy pants. But she's a teacher, she's supposed to wear clothes like that.

"Damn," Jordan whispers. "Where's she been all my life?"

I'm about to tell him there is no possible way a seventh grader can date a teacher (I watch the news—that only happens in high school), when I realize that's not who he's talking about.

I follow Jordan's gaze and see *her*.

Walking across the front of the room is the most beautiful girl I've ever seen. She's tan, has straight pitch-black hair, and is wearing a kelly green shirt. She's also got one of those tiny backpacks, so small it looks like a miniature purse dangling in the center of her back. Below that, a long white skirt swishes as she moves. In a word, she's hot.

In more words, she's smoking, scorching, ultra-spicy-State-Fair-chili-with-jalapenos-and-habaneros-and-both-kinds-of-Tabasco-bubbling-in-a-cast-iron-pot hot.

Ms. Fernandez looks at her watch. "Class starts at 8:05. Sharp."

"Sorry. I—I have a note."

Head down, the hot girl walks to Ms. Fernandez, hands her the note. Then the girl turns and looks for a seat. All the guys in the room are silent. A couple rows back, I hear Zee mutter to Jordan:

"Hello? What are *you* staring at?"

The hot girl heads across the room, skirt swishing, and down the first row—to the seat right beside me. Sweat beads on my forehead. I try to glance casually at the wall and her at the same time. I hope I don't look cross-eyed.

The girl taps me on the shoulder.

Yes, that's right. She taps my shoulder. As in, touches me. As in, puts one of her perfect fingers on my shirt. As in, I didn't realize my shoulder could feel nervous.

"Is this seat taken?" she whispers.

Up close, I notice her eyes. They are green green green. Like if you took an apple Jolly Rancher and held it up to the sun. That kind of green. Or like on the baseball field, when the grass is long and it rains but then the sun comes out right after, so bright it hurts a little, and shines straight down on the long wet grass, so hard it seems to glow, like green fire. That's what her eyes are like.

Still half-looking at the wall, I mumble what I hope is a "No," and make what I hope is a shaking motion with my head.

She drops her mini backpack and sits down. In the seat. Beside *me*!

Okay. Some guys may be used to stuff like this: goddess-like creature walks in room, looks around, picks desk by them. I'm sure there are guys this happens to every day. Those guys are not me.

It's not like I'd get voted "Most Hideous," but fact-check: I'm two inches shorter than most guys, two inches wider on the sides, have blonde hair that refuses to do anything but poof out like a space helmet, and I get sunburned about 1.35 seconds after leaving the shade.

I am basically the chick anti-magnet.

But right now, none of that matters. Ms. Fernandez is going around the room doing intros, but I'm not listening; I'm sneaking glances at the desk beside me.

The girl with green-apple eyes is wearing white sandals, her toenails painted orange with white swirls, like little comets. She's got a light red splotch on the top of her left foot—it looks like a birthmark, or like she forgot to put sunscreen on that spot for a week. But hey, nobody's 100 percent perfect, right? I put her at about 99 percent.

99 percent runs a hand through the back of her shiny-black hair, and I swear I can smell vanilla. I love vanilla. Make that 99.9 percent.

"Yo yo yo," Jordan whispers behind me. "I'm Jordan. Where'd you move from?"

Hey, what's he doing? She sat next to *me*! I turn and glare, but Jordan isn't paying attention. His outstretched leg is kicking at the new girl's sandal.

She stands. "I'm Angela Savory," she says to the room. "We just moved here from Memphis, Tennessee."

Tennessee? They have the same colors as The University of Texas (orange and white), and the same initials (UT)—I've always thought they were such copycats. But, I guess that also means we have a ton in *common* with Tennessee. They're practically our sister state. Or city. Or something like that. And the new girl is from there? That's pretty cool.

As Angela Savory from Tennessee sits back down, Jordan kicks at her sandal again and smiles, but she shoots him a glare.

Good—serves him right.

I mean, what's he doing, trying to hit on her? He's already dating Zee, the girl sitting right behind him. And what kind of line is "Yo yo yo"? Sounds like something a caveman would come up with: "Yo yo yo, me Jordan. You Angie. Me likey." I still wonder how he got into Honors English. I picture Jordan wearing a Tarzan suit, trying to lift Angela Savory over his shoulder. He could probably do it, easy.

"Yo, brain freeze," Jordan whispers.

16

Suddenly I realize the room is quiet. And everyone is staring at me. Including Angela. Did I mention her eyes are green?

I stand. "I, uh, my name is Chance Peters." The perspiration kicks into second gear on my forehead.

"We just moved here from … I mean, no—we're *from* here."

Somebody giggles. A sweat bead rolls down, tickles its way out of my hair, and lands in my ear hole with a plop! I can feel it, sitting in there, like a tiny lake. Lake Eardrum.

I shake my head back and forth, trying to drain the lake. Slowly, Angela slides her sandals and practically perfect feet under her desk, away from me.

"This summer, I, uh…"

My brain is melting. All I can focus on is how stupid I look, what Jordan and Zee must be thinking, what Angela must be thinking.

"This summer, uh … it was pretty hot…"

I hear more giggles, all around. After a couple more seconds, Ms. Fernandez asks if I want to continue. Angela is bent over a tiny green notebook, writing, not even looking at me. I shake my head "no" and take a seat.

Brilliant, Chance. Just brilliant.

I am.

Such.

A dork.

Behind me I hear a rustle, a confident cough, then a smooth deep voice.

"Yo. I'm Jordan Vargas…"

I smell cologne—lots of it—as soon as he stands. When did he start wearing *that*?

Collision

Thankfully, Angela isn't in my other classes or my lunch period, so I don't have to try and explain my first period brain implosion. Last period, of course, is football.

We're all gathered in the football locker room, every seventh grade guy at William Nelson Middle. Jordan wasn't kidding—it really is awesome. Everything's shiny-sparkly clean, the walls look like they were painted burnt orange yesterday, and it's ten times brighter than the P.E. locker room. Even the ceiling seems higher. We don't go to church, but I wonder if this is what one looks like inside.

A few minutes earlier, the trainer handed out shoulder pads. Now everyone's sitting in front of their lockers, our names printed above on big pieces of white tape. Mine is next to the new kid's, whose full name is Kevin Spielman. Jordan's locker is on the far side, by an open door filled with sunlight.

The door darkens as a huge man steps in. He's

wearing a burnt orange shirt, tucked firmly into white shorts, and his legs are approximately the size of rocket boosters. He folds his arms together and rows of muscles pop out. His skin is tan and crinkly, like an old baseball glove, like he's been in the sun for fifty years straight. It looks like he's staring straight ahead, but I can't really tell—his eyes are hidden behind orange-reflective sunglasses. His hair is thick and gray. On top of it, a sharp new baseball cap says, HEAD COACH.

No kidding.

"Footballll," Head Coach says, drawing the word wayyyy out. His voice is super low and somehow sounds slow and fast at the same time, like a bowling ball when it rolls down the alley, picking up speed right before it smacks into the pins.

"Footballll," he repeats, "is all about *collision.*" He smashes into the bowling pins on the last word. He doesn't yell, but I can feel his voice, vibrating the center of my chest.

Head Coach scans the room, like he already knows who's good at "collision" and who's not. He turns and I see myself, a tiny reflection in his yellow-orange sunglasses. I look down. Immediately.

"Everyone suit up," Head Coach says. "Shorts and shoulder pads only."

I look over at Jordan, wondering if his football camp this summer was like this, if—

"That means *now*!"

The locker room is a flurry of shirts and pads and shoes. I throw on my cleats and shorts, then yank my shoulder pads over my head, tying them in front; I'm surprised how light they are. Finally I put some sunscreen on my face. I'll burn to crisp if I don't.

"I like your cleats."

Beside me, Kevin Spielman is adjusting his shoulder pads. They look about five sizes too big.

"Uh, thanks."

My cleats are from baseball this summer and they're maroon. I need to get Mom to take me for some football ones (black). That's the current #4 on my list.

Kevin takes out a pair of cleats so white they seem to glow. I watch as he threads one with bright green laces. Then he puts electric blue laces on the other shoe.

"I'm going to rotate the colors everyday," he says. "I figure, why have boring feet, right? Tomorrow, I'm thinking red and yellow."

Does he not realize how serious football is? I'm already worried about my cleats, since maroon is not one of our colors. Head Coach will probably cream Kevin for wearing those laces. Not to mention what the other guys on the team will do. It makes me kind of nervous, just sitting next to him.

Kevin leans down to tie his shoes, but his shoulder pads are so big he can barely reach. He stretches, grunts, twists sideways a couple times, and finally gets the cleats tied.

Suddenly I realize the locker room is empty. We're late.

Crap.

"There are many things I don't tolerate," Head Coach says when Kevin and I reach the practice field. "One of them, is lateness."

Head Coach seems even bigger outside. He's holding a football, palming the entire thing in one hand. The other guys are on the ground behind him, stretching. Jordan is doing some crazy stretch with his arms and legs all mixed together.

"Sorry, sir," Kevin says. "It was my—"

"Another thing I don't tolerate, *Spielman*," Head

Coach says, "are excuses."

Kevin shuts up.

Wait—Head Coach already knows Kevin's name?

"Yes, *Peters*," he says, as if he can read my mind, "I know all your names."

From the corner of my eye, I see Jordan punch a tall guy in the arm and whisper. The tall guy is Linden Cole, but he just goes by Cole. I don't know why. Maybe he hates his first name. I don't think Linden's so bad, but whatever. Everyone calls him Cole. Even his teachers.

I notice Cole's wearing the same shorts as Jordan, from summer football camp. I also notice he looks like he's gained about fifty pounds since last year, all muscle. Cole nods at whatever Jordan just said, then laughs.

What did Jordan tell him? Was he making fun of Kevin's laces? Of Head Coach? Of—

Head Coach's bowling-ball voice stops me mid-thought: "*Vargas! Cole!*"

Jordan and Cole sit up, stop laughing.

Head Coach points the football at them. "Another thing I don't tolerate, is laughing during practice. Unless it's at my jokes."

I wait for him to share one of his jokes, or maybe at least smile, but Head Coach just stands there.

In the distance, the locusts start up; it sounds like a thousand rattlesnakes, all shaking at the same time, going faster and faster, until they finally end in a fever pitch. I feel the sweat on my head, armpits, chest. The sun is out in full force now. The air smells like burnt grass.

"You four!"

Head Coach's voice snaps. He points the football at me, Kevin, Jordan and Cole. Then he motions to the far end of the field.

"Sprints. To the endzone and back. *Now*."

We all take off running.

Fact-check: You couldn't tell from looking at me, but I can run fast.

Really fast.

At first it's a little strange, running with the shoulder pads on. They make me go a bit side-to-side, like I'm waddling. But they're not heavy at all, and after a couple seconds I straighten out my stride, barely notice them. I catch up to Jordan and Cole. Kevin is at least ten yards behind.

Cole spits off to the side. "Thanks a ton, *Peters*." He says my last name like it's some inside joke.

I want to tell him it's not my fault he got in trouble—Jordan's the one who made him laugh. But I don't say anything. I just speed up, passing him. Jordan's still with me.

"Damn, Jordan," Cole calls from behind, "you've got some speed!"

Hey, why does he call Jordan by his first name, but not me? And what about *my* speed? Can't he see we're running side-by-side?

Jordan goes a little faster. "Oh, yeah," he says. I can't tell if he's answering Cole, or making some manly statement to me.

I catch up, my short legs churning like pistons, Jordan's longer legs striding out, graceful. For every step he takes, I probably take three. When we raced this summer at Barton Springs pool, the kids called us "the pit bull and the Chihuahua." I was the Chihuahua. (And I won.)

We reach the endzone and turn back, passing Cole and then Kevin. Kevin's left shoelace is undone, a flapping string of bright blue around his ankle. A few seconds later, I hear Cole making fun of him: "Nice laces, Freak Zone."

Jordan is running full speed now. He glances sideways and opens his mouth, like he's about to speak. Maybe he'll tell me what he said to Cole earlier. But then his mouth closes and he looks forward again, doesn't say anything.

It's weird. Jordan's been my best friend for two years, but sometimes I just don't get him. Maybe it's because he's not really big on the using-words thing.

I think about him on the bus with Zee, not telling me about her or about his new clothes. Then I think about him in first period, hitting on Angela Savory. I speed up, my feet moving so fast they barely touch the ground. I leave Jordan behind; I wish Angela were here to see.

So what if Jordan's hanging out with Zee and Cole? At least I'm still faster than him. I wonder if Angela likes Chihuahuas.

Suddenly I hear footsteps behind me. The next thing I know, Jordan's at my side again.

What the?

We're at mid-field, fifty yards to go. I'm pumping

my legs and arms as hard as I can; sweat flings from my hair onto my face, into my eyes; my hands slice the air, cutting the heat and humidity and dust. All around me, the world is a stream of color, brown grass and blue sky and yellow-fire sun. I'm sprinting as fast as I ever have.

And Jordan is matching me, step for step.

Twenty-five yards to go.

The other guys are cheering us from the endzone. Head Coach is holding a stop-watch, just like Dad used to when I was a kid, when he'd time me racing across our backyard.

Suddenly I want nothing more in the world than to finish first, to show Head Coach how fast I am, that I'm the fastest in my class, fastest in the whole state of Texas. I want to make him proud.

I push myself as hard as I can. I am a blur of speed, a milli-second ahead of Jordan.

Ten yards to go.

Jordan's shoulder pad collides with mine, forcing me to take a stutter-step to the side. Did he do that on purpose?

Five yards left.

I try to right myself, get back in stride. Jordan

glides past, finishes just ahead of me.

Head Coach clicks the stopwatch button. "Nice work, Vargas."

Crap.

Long Distance

"How was your first day?"

This is how Mom greets me as I plop into the front seat of our car, after practice. She's still wearing her work outfit: a starched white lab coat with Martha O'Neill (her name) and D.D.S. (her way to say dentist) stitched across the front. I picture myself wearing the same thing: Chance Peters, D.D.S. Dumb Dateless Student.

Mom pulls onto the main road, away from school. I consider telling her about my brain meltdown in English, but then I'd probably have to mention Angela Savory. Mom and I have never had one (1) single conversation about girls, and I do *not* feel like starting now. I also think about mentioning how Jordan was wearing all new clothes, is dating Zee Mays, and beat me in a race but maybe cheated by knocking into my shoulder pad, but I don't feel like talking about any of that either.

"Fine," I say.

We're stopped at a light. Mom gives me a look. "Sounds thrilling," she says.

What does she want, a minute-by-minute recap of the entire day?

"Sorry," Mom says, "I didn't mean to make fun, I'm just a little…"

She twists her hands on the wheel, like she's wringing a towel. "Your dad called," she says.

My first instinct is to let out a half-laugh and try to change the subject. But I just sit there, the seatbelt pinching my chest like a roller coaster with the bar pulled too tight. The last time I heard from Dad was four months ago, when he called to make sure I'd gotten the football he sent for my birthday.

"Somehow," Mom says, "he remembered it was your first day of school. He left a message on the machine." She's staring straight ahead.

"Oh," is all I can think to say.

The rest of the short ride home is quiet. When we get inside, I glance at the answering machine. The light's not blinking.

"I already listened to it," Mom says. "It's the only

message on there."

The "Play" button is right next to "Delete." For a second I'm not sure which to hit.

The machine clicks and Dad's scratchy smoker voice comes from the speaker. "Hello, Mr. High School!" A little chuckle. "Just kidding, I know it's only seventh grade, but you'll be done with middle school before you know it! Anyway, I was hoping to catch you, but maybe you're still asleep, since you're two hours earlier than out here and…" A pause, a bit too long. "Oh, wait, you're two hours *later*. Man, I always get that wrong." Another chuckle, a bit too rehearsed. "Well, I'm sure it's great, I bet you're already first-string running back, and first in your class, too—" A woman yells something in the background and Dad's voice is muffled, like his hand's over the phone. Then he's back, without the muffle. "Okay, Chance, gotta go. Good luck out there, Mr. High School!"

I wait for something more, but that's it. No words of wisdom, no call-me-back-Chance, nothing. I pick up the phone receiver and look at the caller ID, but there's only a "Blocked" call listed.

Why didn't he leave a number? Maybe he was

going to, but then he had to hang up in a hurry. Or maybe

he wanted it to be a challenge, to see if I could find his

number on my own, to see if I'm the smartest kid in my

class. My mind races, thinking how I could look it up,

but then I stop.

This is stupid. If he'd wanted to leave a number,

he would have.

I notice my hand is warm, still clutching the

phone receiver. I put it back down.

Mom sighs beside me. "So," she says, "how

about we get chili?"

*   *   *

We order my favorite—the "Pepper Piñata" from

Texas Chili Parlor, super-spicy chili covering a hidden

surprise of tortilla chips, three different cheeses, and three

different hot peppers.

"I'm sorry, Chance."

Mom is staring at me, a glass of tea in her hand.

I'm pretty sure she's talking about Dad. Again. I stab

into my chili piñata, get a fork-full of cheese and peppers.

"Chance, I'm sorry your dad is so… He didn't

always used to be like that."

I take a huge bite, let the spices sizzle in my

mouth. Why can't we just eat?

"Chance? You know it's not your fault, right? Your dad and I splitting up, you know it had nothing to do with you, right?"

"Uh-huh."

She's only told me this about fifty thousand times before. Of course it wasn't because of me. Not that I remember it or anything. I take another bite; it's so spicy my tongue is feeling numb.

"And him leaving," Mom says, "moving away. That's…"

She looks sad, her eyes heavy, like they're going to slide down her face.

"Sometimes, Chance, people just change."

I think about Jordan's new clothes, new friends, new everything. Tell me about it.

I wonder if Mom's changed, too. Or if she's going to change. I swallow a big gulp of chili; I can barely taste it anymore but I still feel it, going all the way down. My stomach is stuffed but empty at the same time; I feel sick.

"I think I'm full," I say. "Can I go do homework?"

Mom stares at me with those heavy eyes. Then she nods her head and I'm up and away from the table, straight to my room.

I shut the door and flop onto my bed. I toss my baseball in the air, catch it in my other hand when it comes down, then flip it back to my throwing hand. Toss, catch-and-flip. Toss, catch-and-flip. Like I've done millions of times.

The football Dad gave me is on my shelf. I should practicing throwing that, now that I'm actually playing. But I don't really want to get up.

I toss the baseball higher. It almost hits the ceiling, which is covered with the glow-in-the-dark stars I put up there years ago. The big star right above me is Dad; I picture him out in California, not leaving a number. The shooting star is Head Coach, shaking his head at me as I come in second. Those three, crammed close together like a constellation, are Jordan, Zee and Cole. And all the others, spread out across the ceiling in perfect pairs, are the rest of my class.

Things aren't supposed to be like this.

I drop the baseball on the floor, then grab my phone and call Jordan. But it just rings and rings, then goes to voicemail—he must be eating dinner. (Jordan's parents don't let him have the phone at the table, just like Mom does with me.) I listen to Jordan's message *("Yo, it's me. Do it at the beep.")*, but can't think of exactly what I want to say. I hang up before it starts recording. Maybe I'll try him later, or maybe he'll call after they're done eating.

I unfold my blue To-Do list, hoping it'll help me figure things out, but for once that doesn't work. Why not? Is it missing something? Is there something I forgot to—

Of course! I leap from my bed, turn on my computer, and pull up my Main To-Do list. At the top, I type:

#1. GET A GIRLFRIEND

I'd mentally added it this morning, but it feels better to actually write it, to see the words on the screen. Already my stomach is settling back to normal.

Okay. I can do this, I just have to think it through: How do I get a girlfriend?

The answers come so easy, I don't know why I didn't think of them before:

#1a. get new clothes

#1b. get better at football (fast)

Plus, the second one will impress Head Coach. Bonus points.

I'll ask Mom to take me shopping for the clothes. For football, I'll check out some books at the library, start doing sprints on the weekends. Perfect.

But, I still need to figure out *who*. I can't just start going out with anyone—that would defeat the whole purpose. I need a girlfriend everyone likes. A girlfriend who is as close to perfect as…

I look at a comet on my ceiling. Then I picture a comet-swirl toenail, green-apple eyes, all the guys in first period silent as she looks for a seat, and Jordan kicking her sandal. How could it be anyone else? I type another line:

#1c. go out with A.S.

And I know exactly how to make it happen. The next time I talk to her, I won't stumble and stutter and sweat like I did in first period. No, I'll be calm and cool, say exactly the right things. Exactly.

I have a plan.

"Kevin on the bus"

<u>The Plan, phase I</u>: Observation.

The next day, Tuesday, I'm a world-class spy. During first period, instead of listening to Ms. Fernandez discuss our homework ("In one page, describe your first memory"), I'm stealing glances at Angela Savory. She's hunched over her mini notebook, writing with her hand a little crooked, but even that looks perfect. Today she's wearing a light blue shirt (my favorite color!), a denim skirt and flip-flops, and has the same orange-swirl toenails, same left-foot birthmark, same vanilla smell from her hair. I think vanilla may be my new favorite flavor.

<u>Phase II</u>: Research.

In study hall, I look up everything possible on birthmarks, Tennessee and Memphis. Over the summer, I took free computer classes at the library and they're totally paying off—I can find stuff so quick, I think we need a faster connection. I also search for information on green eyes, orange swirls, and vanilla shampoo.

"Hey, whatcha doin?"

Kevin Spielman is at the computer beside me, leaning over. I minimize the screen.

"Research," I say.

"Cool," Kevin says. "I like research."

I nod then stretch back in my seat, trying to look bored.

Kevin sits there, like he's waiting for me to say something.

Finally he goes back to his computer. But not before he's given me another idea. I pull up my screen again, add one more thing, and hit print.

I glide through football practice, not really caring that Wednesday is going to be "full contact" day. I have more important things to think about. And her initials are A.S.

Phase III: Synthesis.

At home, I go straight to my room. I flip on my computer, take out all the info I've collected, and make lists. Revise the lists. Cross-reference the lists. Add in some current events, movie quotes, and a few jokes I find online, just in case. Then I cull it down to one master list.

The List.

It's almost dinnertime. I take a seat on my bed and look over the printout. It's got everything I could possibly say, every interesting question, every funny comment, for every situation. It's 99.9 percent perfect. Just like A.S.

I look her up in the class directory. For a second, I think about texting or emailing, so I can write everything out exactly the way I want, make sure I get it just right. But if I send her something, she might not see it for a while. I remember all the guys in first period checking her out. I bet the same thing happened in her other classes, too. What if some other guy calls her first and asks her out?

Nope, I definitely have to call. Tonight.

I practice my introduction. "Angela? Hey, it's Chance Peters. You know, the dorky guy who sits beside you in first period? [pause for laughs] Yeah, um, so anyway, uh…"

Way too wimpy.

I clear my throat. Think confident, think cool.

I am an iceberg. I am the country of Iceland. I am the entire cast of Disney on—

"Chance?" There's a knock on my door. "Dinner

in ten minutes."

"Okay, Mom."

The floor creaks as Mom walks away. I grab the phone and dial Angela's number before I can talk myself out of it. I take a deep breath, trying to think cool thoughts as I move into the final phase of my plan.

<u>Phase IV</u>: Contact.

Ring one.

Ice.

Ring two

Ice cube.

Ring three.

Ice cream—

"Hello?" Angela's voice sounds just as perfect on the phone. And she picked up on ice cream. I love ice cream.

"Angela?" My voice is smooth. Like Blue Bell homemade vanilla.

"Yes?"

"Hey, it's Chance Peters. You know, the dorky guy who sits beside you in first period?"

I chuckle, but all she says is: "Oh." And then: "Hi."

Why didn't she laugh? I'm sure she can. I mean, I've seen her laugh before, right? Okay, I tell myself, don't panic. Go to your strength. Go to The List.

I start with Item #1. "So. We, uh, you sit next to me in first period."

"Um, right. I think you mentioned that."

Crap. Item #1 was the intro. Which I already did. Crap crap crap. This was not part of the plan.

I scan The List, looking for something to save me, and see #3b. Jokes. Perfect!

The first joke is way too complicated, and has to do with birthmarks. Why did I think that would be funny? What if she gets offended?

The second one just says, "Joke about Preparation G." I try to remember it, something about how isn't Preparation H a weird name, and maybe there was a Preparation G right before, and if so that would be funny because—

That has to be the lamest joke ever.

I continue down The List. The next one says, "Kevin on the bus."

My brain flickers in recognition. That was what I remembered earlier, when Kevin Spielman was talking to me in study hall. There was something funny about him on the bus. Maybe he was picking his nose, or tripped on the steps, or wore tight pants, or…

Crap. I really should have put more details in.

"Um, Chance?"

Angela. I'd almost forgotten about her.

"Oh, sorry," I stammer. "I was, uh…"

I stare at The List, but it all blurs together.

"So, hey—did you see Kevin Spielman on the bus today?" I ask.

"No."

"Oh, well, you *totally* should have."

I think back, trying to picture the bus ride. Suddenly, I realize how dumb this is: Angela doesn't even ride my bus. I try to think of something else, but my mind goes cold.

"Yeah," I continue. "Kevin. He was on the *bus*." I say the last word with emphasis, like somehow that will make it a good punch line. It doesn't.

What could've been so funny about him, about Kevin?

"So," I say. "So he was…"

I struggle to remember, but it feels like I'm

thinking slower than a glacier.

"He was … he was *there*…"

Now I can't even remember what I'm supposed to be talking about. All I see is myself, standing in an endless field of snow.

"Chance?"

Wind howls across the empty tundra of my brain.

"Chance, I have to go. We're eating."

"Yeah…"

My mouth is on auto-pilot, dribbling out words like bits of crushed ice.

"He was … he was *on* it…"

I want to stop, but I can't.

"He was right there … right on it … on the … the …"

"Goodbye, Chance."

"Bus?"

The receiver clicks. A few seconds later, the dial tone sounds.

I look at The List. It's crystal-clear now. Miles and miles of perfect, hilarious, more-interesting-than-God-himself things to say.

The phone lets out a high-pitched beep: "If you'd

like to make a call, please hang up and try again…"

Fastball

For a second, I consider doing it: Just hang up and try again.

I can fix this. If I call Angela back—right now—I can tell her it was all a big joke, that I was just about to deliver the superstar, grand finale, knock 'em dead punch line, right before she said goodbye.

"Oh," she'd say. "Cool! I'm so sorry I hung up, Chance. What's the punch line?"

And then I'd tell her the punch line for the great "Kevin on the bus" joke, the funniest thing ever… The punch line where… The one where…

I have no idea.

I hang up the phone and flop on my bed. This is a complete disaster.

I'm lying on my stomach. I feel my heart beating beneath me, going about fifty thousand times a second. It's like I'm a hummingbird or something. I wonder if Angela could hear that on the other end of the phone. It probably sounded like I was playing the drums.

46

Wait—maybe that's why the call didn't go well. Maybe Angela just couldn't hear me, over my super-loud heartbeat. But then I realize how dumb that is. I know exactly why the call bombed: I was talking like a complete idiot. Like my brain had been replaced with a pair of socks.

It sinks in for real now, what just happened. There is no way Angela Savory will ever want to talk to me again. Much less go out with me.

I take out my other list, the one on light blue paper. And I cross out item #1c.

How do other guys do it? How do they all suddenly have girlfriends? Did they all get a manual over the summer?

The Seventh Grade Guide to Dating, Austin Edition: How to Get a Girlfriend in Two Weeks or Less! (Unless Your Name Starts with 'Chance').

Maybe they sent mine to the wrong address. Maybe it's at Dad's, out in California.

Dad. What would he say, if I told him about my call to Angela?

"It's ok, Mr. High School! There's plenty of fish in the sea, you'll catch one in no time!"

"Hey, Mr. High School, don't worry about girls, it's football you gotta focus on!"

"Chance, the most important thing about girls is ... oh, sorry, gotta go! Good luck out there, Mr. High School!"

I roll on my side. Everything in my room looks slanted from this angle, like I'm sideways on a roller coaster at Six Flags. On my desk, I see the photo from when Jordan and I went there, last summer. He's got one arm around my neck and is doing the Texas "hook 'em" sign with his other hand. We're both cracking up. And soaking wet. We'd just gone on the log ride and Jordan sat up front, me right behind. We spent the whole day there. It was perfect.

I grab my phone and dial Jordan's number.

He'll know what to do. I mean, he probably made some mistakes with Zee, right? Especially since, at the start of summer, he had the exact same amount of girl experience as me. (Zero.) I wonder how he and Zee started dating. And when. And why he never said anything.

The phone keeps ringing, then I hear Jordan's voice.

48

"Yo, it's me. Do it at the beep."

"Hey, Jordan, it's me. Hey, um, I was calling because … well, just call me back. Soon. Okay, bye."

I lay on my bed, staring at my phone. Maybe he's going to the bathroom and he'll call back in a couple seconds.

The light on the front screen dims, then goes into sleep mode.

And then it vibrates. Yes! I click it on, but no call. Weird. I swore I felt it, but maybe it was just my hummingbird heart, still nervous from the Angela call. I roll on my back, holding the phone an inch above my face, waiting. The screen goes black again.

On the blank surface, I can barely see my own reflection, staring back. I look like some shadow kid, like I'm in outer space, or maybe trapped in another dimension. I wonder if the other me, in the other world inside my phone, knows how to ask out a girl.

Jordan's got to call back soon. I glance over at the photo on my desk, the one from Six Flags. I remember us standing there together, dripping water.

"Yo, Chance-man," Jordan said, right after his dad

took the photo. "How's that wet arm feeling?"

He pointed up the Midway, to the *Guess Your Speed!* baseball game. My favorite.

"I can out-throw you anytime," I said. "Whether my arm's wet, dry, or sawn off."

"Ha ha—it's on, Chance-man, it's on!"

We sprinted to the game booth, where a heavy plastic tarp with a catcher painted on it hung on the back wall, and a radar gun showed your ball speed.

"You get two practice throws," the vendor told us, "then on your last one—"

"Yeah yeah," Jordan interrupted, "we know. If we guess our speed on the dot, we get a prize."

Jordan and I both threw exactly the same on our first two throws: 52 miles per hour, then 53.

For his last throw, Jordan predicted a 55.

"A fifty-*five!*" The vendor repeated it into a megaphone. A small crowd had gathered around the booth.

Jordan took a quick breath, did his pitching windup, and let go.

54.

"Ohhhhh," the vendor called out, "so close!"

Jordan shrugged. "Yeah, but it's still faster than Chance." He smiled and did a mock-bow.

The vendor turned to me. "So, what's your prediction, son? How fast?"

"55."

"Look at that spirit!" The vendor faced the crowd. "A fifty-five—same as his friend!"

I walked to the throwing spot, staring at the catcher like he was real. I tossed the ball from one hand to the other, feeling its perfect weight, the rough stitching, the grooves that seemed made just for my fingers. I imagined an actual batter, waiting for my pitch. And I pictured myself, throwing a blazing fastball right by him, so hard it made the catcher's glove smack like fireworks.

And then I did it.

55.

The crowd gave me a smattering of applause.

Jordan shook his head, then smiled. "Guess the radar doesn't lie, huh? But you know, C-man, baseball's not really my sport..."

"Yeah yeah," I said. "Excuses, excuses."

When the vendor asked what prize I wanted I didn't think twice: the huge stuffed football with a

Longhorns logo, hanging at the front of the booth. The vendor handed it to me, but I immediately tossed it to Jordan.

For a second Jordan was surprised, then he caught it and broke into a goofy grin. "Excellent choice, C-man, excell—"

A loud knock startles me back to the present.

"Chance?"

It's Mom, knocking on my bedroom door.

"Chance? Dinner's ready."

"Ok," I call out, still looking at the picture of me and Jordan.

Why does that seem like so long ago? And why didn't we go to Six Flags this summer, before Jordan left for football camp? I try to remember if it even came up. But I'm having a hard time thinking straight—the Angela phone call has turned my brain inside-out. I really, really need to talk to Jordan.

I check the phone again—nothing—then put it on my desk, next to the photo.

At the table, I gulp down my spaghetti and milk. Should I give Jordan a play-by-play of the whole Angela

52

call? No, I should just tell him I was an idiot, but leave out the specifics. That'll be better than going through my entire List, plus Jordan probably won't be interested in every single little detail about—

"Chance? You should try and take a breath between bites."

"Mmmhhm, ssrry."

"Chance, is everything all right?"

Mom puts her fork down. It hits her plate with a soft clink.

Should I tell her what happened? Maybe she'd have some great, perfect, motherly advice. But what would I say? And where would I start? I'd have to tell her about Angela, about all the other guys having girlfriends, about everything.

I look at Mom. She's got a spaghetti noodle dangling from her chin, like a one-whisker beard. No, Jordan's the one I need to talk to.

"I'm fine," I say. "I just … we have a lot of homework."

Mom stares at me for a couple seconds, then nods. "Okay, honey."

I'm done eating in less than ten minutes, then

back in my room.

I rush to the desk, check my phone. There's a text! From Jordan!

Yo. Busy now, but chat mañana.

Busy? What's he busy with? Is he hanging out with Zee? With Cole? And he can't talk until tomorrow? How am I supposed to wait that long to figure out what to do about Angela? I want to call back and ask all of that, but instead I just send a message:

Ok.

Kevin. On the Bus.

The next morning, the bus is a few minutes late. And crowded. The bus driver, looking grouchy, apologizes and tells me they're combining routes.

I walk back to where Jordan and Zee are sitting together. Cole is in the seat across from them—he must have been on the other route, the one we combined with today. And he's got his arm around Jessica Stoddard, a cheerleader.

"Well, if it isn't Mr. Public Speaking himself," Cole says.

My face is suddenly on fire. Did Angela tell everyone about my call? Already?

Cole's voice is mocking: "This summer, uh … it was, uh, like, totally *hot*."

It takes me a second to realize he's making fun of me from yesterday, from first period; he doesn't know about the call. Which makes me feel better. Slightly. Except that Cole's not in Honors English—which means someone else told him what happened yesterday morning.

"Yo, Chance man!" Jordan shoots a punch at me. Did *he* tell Cole? I picture the two of them, whispering together in football practice.

Beside him, Zee is staring over a book. But she's not giving me her all-knowing look; instead, her head is tilted a little, like she's curious.

"Hey, Chance," she says.

"No standing, kid!" the bus driver calls from up front. "You need to take a seat."

I look around, but the bus is full. I really wish I weren't the last stop.

"Up here," the driver calls. In the very front seat, Kevin Spielman scoots over. Jordan says something to Cole, they both laugh. Zee flicks him in the ear.

I scan the bus, one last time, hoping to see a spare seat. And that's when I notice a head of smooth black hair, bent over a little green notebook, near the very back. My belly suddenly feels like it's full of super-bounce rubber-balls, all ricocheting off each other and slamming into the sides of my stomach and my intestines (both upper and lower):

Angela Savory is on my bus.

She must have been on the other route, too, the

one with Cole. She's still got her head down, writing in her notebook. I hope hope hope and pray she hasn't noticed me. How can I possibly face her, after my call last night? If she looked up right now, I'd probably pee my pants. Or worse.

I do a quick 180 and head up front. I take the seat beside Kevin.

For a couple seconds I just sit there, catching my breath as the driver puts the bus in gear and we move forward. Once we get to school I can race off, make sure there's no way she sees me. Maybe I'll even duck down. Yes, I'll definitely duck.

I glance in the huge rearview mirror over the driver's head, just to make sure Angela's still not looking. I lean forward, trying to get the right angle, but I can't see back far enough.   Kevin Spielman is beside me, staring.

"Hey," I say quickly. I'm still nervous from seeing Angela.

"Hi," Kevin says. "Beautiful day, isn't it?"

"Yeah. Sure."

It's sunny, hazy, and humid. Like always.

I notice Kevin's not wearing the puffy space

jacket today. (The jacket, of course, was what I meant to joke about with Angela last night. But I push that to the very back of my brain.) Today, Kevin's in a bright green T-shirt that says I LOVERMONTPELIER across the front.

"It's the capital," he says.

Huh?

"Montpelier," Kevin continues, as if I'd actually asked. "It's the capital of Vermont." He looks straight down at his own chest, points. "The last two letters of LOVE are the first two of VERMONT. And the last four letters of VERMONT are the first four of—"

"I get it."

"Pretty cool, huh?"

Actually, it is. But it's not something I'd ever wear to school. Or anywhere.

"It's also the smallest state capital," Kevin continues, "at least population-wise. At least in the United States. I bet there's smaller ones in other countries. I need to look that up."

He takes out a sheet of paper and writes INT'L CAPS on it.

"So how many do you think there are?" he asks.

58

"What?"

"People. In Montpelier."

"I have no idea. Fifty thousand?"

"No way!" Kevin says. "Not even *close!*"

I really wish he wouldn't yell. I glance in the big rearview mirror again.

"In Montpelier," he says, "there are only *seven* thousand people! Can you imagine, living in a town that small? Austin has over seven *hundred* thousand. And we're a capital, too."

"Yes, I know. I live here."

"Right right right. I wasn't trying to say you were dumb or anything like that. But we haven't covered it in Texas History yet, so I wasn't sure. A lot of people probably think it's Dallas. Or Houston."

Who would think that? How could anyone not know Austin is the capital? But then I remember Kevin just moved here. I try to remember where he said he was from, but I draw a blank. I start to ask, but then he'd probably think I was trying to be his friend. I turn and stare out the front window.

"I wore the shirt because of our English essay," Kevin says. "The one where we write about our first memory."

Oh holy crap—I completely forgot about our assignment!

"Mine's about Montpelier," Kevin continues. "We went there when I was four and I got stung by a bee on my grandpa's farm. It got me right on my big toe, at the knuckle part. 'Knuckle stings make you tough,' Grandpa said. 'They make you a man.' What's your essay about?"

I'm so flustered I can barely think. I have never, ever, forgotten an assignment—much less not turned one in. And now I'm about to start seventh-grade Honors English with a zero.

I try to think of my first memory, but all I can see is Kevin's bright green shirt…

I close my eyes. Come on, Chance, think of *something*! I scramble around in my memory cells, searching. The cells stretch out forever, rolling hills and fields. I run across them, looking for buried treasure, but only dig up weeds and rocks.

Why can't I think of anything??

And then, for some reason, my brain fixes itself on Monday, two days ago, the first day of school. I try to make it go somewhere else, but the dumb thing's stuck. Great. We'll be at school in less than five minutes.

I yank out my notebook and start writing. My hand is flying across the paper so fast that the words are out almost as soon as I think them. It's like I'm sprinting, but with a pencil.

I'm still writing as the bus pulls up to school. I race off, ducking just in case, skip my locker and run straight to first period. No one is here. Good. I skid smoothly into my desk seat, like I'm sliding into third base. I keep writing, finish just when the bell rings. Whew.

It's not my first memory—obviously—but at least it's *a* memory. I pray Ms. Fernandez doesn't want to read any of them out loud.

She doesn't. Instead, she wants *us* read them out loud.

She calls on me first.

My First Memory

by Chance Peters

(Honors English, First Period, Ms. Fernandez)

I remember colors. I am sitting there and then she walks in, full of colors.

The first one is when she touches my shoulder, just a finger. The spot on my shirt turns clear orange, like fire. And then it changes to the color of vanilla ice cream, of stars, of swirling comets. Can your skin feel happy? Mine did.

And then I hear her voice. It's like smooth shiny gold. It reminds me of buttons on Dad's suit, when he polishes them so clean they flicker and flash. She asks if she can sit by me, and it's like gold can talk.

The last color is her eyes. They are green, but not the regular kind. Her kind of green sparkles in the sun, but it's mixed with every other color—like a green sky that is full full full of kites, all spinning and twirling bits of color, red rockets, blue snow cones, yellows and purples and everything else, all mixed into the green.

Her green.

I hear a different voice, someone else, calling me from far away. But I'm still looking at all the pretty colors.

A.S.!

I finish reading and collapse into my seat.

Oh King of Crap! Everyone *has* to know it's about Angela! I can't believe I wrote about her, about the first day of school. Why couldn't I remember anything else? And why, at the end, did I have to say "all the pretty colors?"

I can only imagine how much Cole will make fun of me when he hears about *this*. I slink down, as far as I can go.

"Thank you, Chance," Ms. Fernandez says. "Your use of metaphor and simile verged on being poetic. And your essay overall was very sincere."

She totally knows, doesn't she? Ms. Fernandez knows it wasn't my first memory at all.

And I bet she's making me fun of me, secretly, by saying it's "sincere." Sincere? That's like saying something is "interesting." Like saying, "that's possibly the most boring, lame, corndog of an essay I've ever heard."

64

I stare my desk, waiting for the giggles or out-right laughs, but don't hear any. Maybe Ms. Fernandez is giving the whole class a "leave him alone" look. Or maybe I've gone deaf from reading something so ridiculously bad.

Why didn't I work on the essay last night? Why didn't I think about it, edit it, make it about something cool—and something earlier than two days ago—like Dad taking me to a UT football game, or teaching me to dive off the board at Barton Springs pool, or maybe even me and Dad working through my first CYOA book together?

But I know exactly why I didn't write it last night. And it's not a why, it's a who. And that who is sitting right beside me, with the initials A.S. I can't believe how bad my plan nose-dived last night. After the call, I forgot about pretty much everything. And I still haven't looked at her today, haven't come within a hemisphere of making eye contact.

She's probably going to ask Ms. Fernandez if she can switch seats. I bet she's writing it in her notebook this very moment—a formal petition to move to the other side of the room, as far away from me as possible:

Dear Ms. Fernandez:

I am writing to request a seat change. As you know, I currently sit next to Chance Allen Peters. As you also may know, I made this choice myself, on the first day of school. At that time, however, I did not know anything about Chance. He seemed quiet, smart, and maybe even a little cute — in a fifth-grade, still-has-some-baby-fat, could-be-my-little-brother way. So I sat beside him. But then, well, you heard his introduction. He couldn't even remember where he was from! Which wasn't too bad, really, until he called me last night. He was quite awkward, and started making fun of another new student, Kevin Spielman. I don't think it's appropriate to mock one's classmates. (Maybe it's okay if it's a really funny joke, but Chance's wasn't.) So now, I would prefer to move to a different desk, preferably one in the back. Or perhaps next to Kevin, the other new student. Or even in the hall would be better. I wouldn't mind listening through the door, as long as I don't have to sit beside Chance.

Sincerely,

I look over to see how much she's got done, and freeze.

A.S. is staring straight at me.

And then, something miraculous happens: A.S. gives me a smile.

It's a real, honest, ear-to-ear smile. Her eyes light up—even more than usual—and it's like the sun is shining at me through a green kite.

I try to smile back, but I can't even tell if I'm breathing.

A second later her head is down again, bent over her tiny notebook, and she's writing. But I don't care what she's writing now. There's only one thing I can think about:

A smile!

I feel warm, but this time it's a good warm, like the sun hitting you right when you get out of the pool.

Maybe she didn't realize the essay was about her. It never said her name. And for all she knows, there are tons of girls with green eyes who've tapped my shoulder. (Actual count = 1.) Or maybe she actually liked the phone call last night. Maybe, just possibly, she thought the whole Kevin-on-the-bus thing was some crazy, weird joke I made up. A joke that didn't even *need* a punch line.

A smile!

Maybe A.S. doesn't think I'm the biggest stalker-freak on the entire planet. Maybe, just maybe, my plan worked.

A smile!

I open my backpack and take out my latest CYOA book, *Choose Your Own Adventure – Space & Beyond.* Inside is my folded piece of light blue paper, my Main To-Do List. I open the list and add back what I crossed out last night:

#1c. go out with A.S.

Hey, know what else starts with A.S.?

A ☺ !

CYOA

I got my first CYOA two Christmases ago. Mom and Dad had split up a long time before, but he was still living in Austin then, just across town.

"This was my favorite book when I was your age," Dad said as I unwrapped it.

It was a paperback, worn on the edges, with a picture of a knight-wizard on the cover, holding a sword and surrounded by purples and reds and yellows and greens. I loved it. *Choose Your Own Adventure – The Cave of Time.*

Dad and I spent hours reading it. The story starts when a kid in fifth grade (just like I was, back then) discovers this magic cave that takes him to all different time periods, from back to the dinosaurs, to way in the future. And every few pages, we got to make a choice. Like this:

You are standing in a huge cavern, with passages leading left and right. Do you:

Go left? (Turn to p. 33)

Go right? (Turn to p. 70)

Yell out, and see what happens? (Turn to p. 11)

Eat a cheese sandwich? (Turn to p. 150)

Each choice took you to a different page, and more choices, until finally you got to an ending. And there were probably twenty, thirty, maybe forty *different* endings!

Dad and I read each ending together. And then I picked the best one, where the kid goes to ancient Egypt and saves the queen, which saves the whole civilization, which changes history. I circled all the choices that led to that one.

After that, I read it over and over, always to the same ending.

Before he left, Dad gave me a couple other CYOA books for my birthday, and we sat down and worked through those too, finding the best ending and circling the choices for it.

A year ago, Dad moved to California. After that, he never got me another CYOA book. That was also when he stopped calling as much.

But that hasn't stopped me. Sometimes I get

Mom to take me to the used bookstore, and a couple times she's even ordered them online. That's how I got my latest one, *Space & Beyond*. It came in the mail just before school started, just before Jordan came back from football camp. Just before I met Angela Savory.

Angela Savory, who smiled at me this morning.

Now, sitting in the library during study hall, I flip to the earmarked page. My favorite ending so far is where the world is about to die from overcrowding, but a kid finds a distant planet people can live on, and the population moves there and he saves everyone. I turn back to the last choice and pick a new one. When I flip to the new page, it says my spaceship is now approaching a green planet.

Green. Maybe this planet has a bunch of people with green eyes, and a girl with the initials A.S.

Maybe this will be my new best ending.

Full Contact

In last period, we have our first "full contact" football practice.

The trainer gives us helmets, along with pants that hold pads to protect our knees, thighs, and butts. With everything on, I feel like an astronaut suited up and ready to take on the universe.

On the field, Head Coach assigns us positions.

"*Peters*. You're on offense. Running back."

Sweet! He does think I'm fast!

Jordan gets put at running back, too. Cole is on defense, linebacker. Kevin is on special teams, the guys who only come in for kickoffs and punts.

Head Coach has the special teams practice first. They do a few kickoffs. To my surprise, Kevin Spielman isn't half bad. He's not fast, but he's got a knack for getting in people's way and tripping them up. In football, that can be a really good thing.

I'm standing next to Jordan and Cole, watching special teams line up for another play.

"Hey J," Cole says. "Play again tonight, same time?"

"Totally," Jordan says.

I look over at Jordan. He's watching the field.

"Play what?" I ask.

"Oh, just this game," Jordan says, "it's—"

"Freaking awesome!" Cole cuts in. "Best game ever—*World Football Domination!* We played the last three nights against some guys in Madrid! And last night, we finally kicked their butts!"

"Oh," I say. "Cool."

Then I remember last night, right after the Angela call, when I left Jordan a message and told him I needed to chat, that it was important. And he told me he was "busy."

"They gave us free copies in football camp," Jordan says to me. "It's pretty cool. I played from my house, and Cole from his." He grins at me, then punches my arm. "Dude, you need to get your mom to buy a game system!"

I rub my arm.

I wonder if maybe I could ask Dad for a game system for Christmas. I also wonder why Jordan didn't just ask me to come over and play on his system with him. Maybe then I could have talked to him about my phone call, about how I totally messed things up with Angela.

But then I picture her smile, and realize things aren't completely messed up. And maybe it all happened for a reason: If I'd gone over to Jordan's, or even talked to him, things would've been different. I'm not sure how, but maybe if I'd done something else, like tried to call Angela back, she never would have smiled at me this morning.

So, I'm still a little mad at Jordan for last night, but there's no reason to actually say something about it.

"Offense!"

Head Coach's rumble-voice makes us all jump.

"Offense, left side! Defense, on the right!"

We rush to put our helmets on, go to our sides of the field. On offense, Head Coach puts me and Jordan at the two running back slots. He huddles the whole offense together, drawing up a play on his white clipboard: Jordan gets the ball and runs to the left side, while I go to the right as a decoy.

We run the play and Jordan takes the ball, makes

it about three yards, breaks a tackle for a few more, then the defense brings him down.

"Not bad," Head Coach says.

The next play is a fake to Jordan and a handoff to me, up the middle. Only when we actually run it, the middle is all clogged up with guys. So I scoot to the outside, go around everyone, and sprint to the endzone, untouched. Yes!

"What the hell was that?"

Head Coach's voice carries all the way to the end of the field.

"The play, *Peters*, was for you to go up the middle." He points to the rest of the offense as I run back. "What do you think all these people, your teammates, were doing? They were blocking for you, creating a space for you to run. But, apparently, you think you're too good for that. That you don't need them."

I feel the heat pressing down on my helmet, pressing out all the oxygen.

"Line it back up," Head Coach says. "Same play."

Crap.

"And defense," Head Coach says, "now that you know exactly where he's going, you think you can tackle him this time?"

Double crap.

We run the play again, but now the middle is even more clogged than before. Without thinking, I dodge to the outside, away from everyone, and head to the endzone. I turn back before I even cross the goal line.

What the heck am I doing?

"Peters!"

Head Coach is livid. If I could see behind his sunglasses, I bet his eyes would physically be on fire. He exhales, looks at me, then says, "Same play."

The offense starts to line up, but Head Coach stops them. "Oh, no no no. Peters here doesn't think he needs you guys. So we'll let him run this one, all by himself."

Triple crap.

Head Coach presses the ball at me and I take it, holding it in one arm and trying to get into my running back stance with the other.

"Hike!"

A swarm of guys in pads and helmets rush at me,

Cole leading the charge. I want to run to the side, straight off the field.

"Up the middle, Peters!" Head Coach yells.

So that's where I go. And get crushed. Actually, crushed doesn't begin to describe it. It's like I'm a baby frog, hopping out of my comfy-cozy pond for the first time, all soft and shiny-cool wet, but I happen to land right on some railroad tracks, and the tracks have been baking in the sun all day so that it feels like I'm instantly sizzled to a frog biscuit. At the same time a train engine comes barreling along, smushing me into flattened fried frog. And the rest of the train comes right after, every car full of lead and coal and whales, rolling over and over me, until I'm nothing but a pile of frog biscuit dust.

The offense comes back and we run a few more plays, but luckily none of them involve me getting the ball.

After practice we're all in the locker room, everyone's showered and getting ready to leave. Head Coach steps into the room, folds his arms. He's still wearing the sunglasses.

"Not a bad practice," he says. "And *Peters*?"

My stomach falls. Is he going to make me run

sprints for what happened? Or run that same play against the whole defense, by myself, right here in the locker room?

"Peters," he continues. "Good job out there. It takes guts to do that play, to do exactly what I told you. My coach did the very same thing to me, my first practice. And now, when you actually *have* an offense helping you, think how much better it'll be."

All of a sudden, I feel fifty thousand feet tall. Here, in front of every guy in the seventh grade, Head Coach told me I did a good job. It's as if God himself just gave me a medal.

Jordan looks over at me, gives me a nod. Even Cole is looking at me different.

"Football isn't easy," Head Coach says. "And it's not for everyone. And if you think today was tough, next week we get serious."

Serious?

"If you don't like it," Head Coach says, "you should leave. Now."

He is palming an entire helmet with one hand. The room is silent and still. There is no way anyone, even an ant, would so much as flinch right now.

"Good," Head Coach says. "Before we—"

Someone flinched.

Team Sport

To my left, Kevin Spielman stands.

"Spielman?" Head Coach cocks his head. It's almost like he can't believe Kevin has moved. Neither can I. The whole room is holding its breath.

Kevin sets his helmet on the bench. "I'm sorry, Coach."

"Sorry for what?"

"I just—I don't really like football."

I swear I see a smile, a smirk, flicker across Head Coach's lips. "Thanks for letting me know." But then he's all business. "Give your equipment to the trainer," he tells Kevin. "And the rest of you, shower up if you're gonna. The locker room's closed in fifteen."

Head Coach walks out to his office. The locker room is quiet, all thinking the same thing I am: Kevin Spielman just quit football.

What the??

Kevin is the first one to break the spell. He sits down, starts taking off his cleats.

80

A second later, Cole yells across the room.

"Ka-ka-ka-Kevin! The kuh-kuh-kuh-Quitter!"

Some of the guys chuckle. Kevin doesn't look up.
He takes off his socks, folds them into a neat pile.

"Spa-spa-spa-Spielman! The sha-sha-sha-
Shitter!"

The whole locker room laughs.

Cole walks over. "Spielman," he says. His voice
is sharp and angry, like he's talking to a dog that's just
chewed his favorite shoe.

Kevin looks up.

Cole is carrying a football—he points it at Kevin,
puts the tip between his eyes.

Suddenly I wish I wasn't right next to Kevin's
locker. What's Cole going to do? He's at least twice
Kevin's size. And what the heck is Kevin thinking? You
don't just quit football. And you definitely don't say you
don't "like" it. That's like the Pope saying he doesn't like
church.

"Spielman," Cole repeats, pulling the ball away
from Kevin's face. He makes an arc with it, motioning
to the whole room. "I don't know where you're from,"
Cole says, "but here, you play football. It's a team sport.

Now, what I think we're gonna—"

"Vermont."

Cole stops mid-arc. "What?"

"Vermont," Kevin says. "That's where I'm from."

What's he doing? Just keep quiet, put your head down, and quit acting so weird.

Cole takes a step closer. I suddenly realize how near I am—I'm practically standing between them. Cole turns to me.

"What's *your* problem, Peters? You gonna stick up for the quitter-shitter? Or maybe you wanna quit too? Hell, the two of you could form your own little team. Goooooo, Team Quit-Shits!" Cole finishes his cheer and stares at me. "Well?"

No way I want any part of this, but what can I do? Should I say something? Not say something? Or is this all some sort of football ritual, something everyone knows about but me? I look over at Jordan, the only guy in the room bigger than Cole. He's standing there watching, arms crossed, like he's waiting to see what I'll do. Why doesn't he say anything?

I take a step back.

"I, uh … I love football," I say. "Totally. And I

don't…"

Beside me, Kevin is still on the bench. One of his legs is shaking.

"I—I don't even know him," I say.

"Good." Cole turns to Kevin again, points the football. "You get a free pass today, Quitter. But if I ever see you in this locker room again, or even near it, you're dead."

Cole walks off.

Beside me, Kevin finishes changing, then takes his equipment out to the trainer's office. I'm pretty sure his leg is still shaking as he walks through the big double-doors, but he doesn't slow down, doesn't turn, doesn't say a word.

"The Game"

On the ride home with Mom after practice, I get a message from Jordan on my phone:

Yo, WFD tonight. Come over?

It takes me a second to piece together that WFD stands for *World Football Domination.* It's the first message I've gotten from Jordan since the "I'm busy" one the other night. I'm so excited I mis-type "yes!" as "yew!" (twice), before I get it right:

Yes! What time?

Jordan responds immediately: *6:30.*

"Hey, Mom? Can I go over to Jordan's for a while tonight?"

Mom is checking her teeth, eyes darting back and forth between the visor mirror and the road.

"Sure, honey." She flips up the visor, glances at me. "You know, you're always welcome to invite Jordan to our place."

"Yeah, I know."

I don't know why Mom always gets on me about

that. Of course I could invite Jordan over. But our place is *way* smaller than the Vargases. And Jordan has cool stuff like a game system (two actually – one for him, one for his older brother), and a basketball hoop in the driveway. If he came over to my place, what would we do? Throw the baseball? Not Jordan's thing. Watch TV on our dinky little set? Jordan's TV is like a movie screen. Read my CYOAs together? Yeah, right.

When we get home Mom makes mac and cheese (from the box, my favorite), I scarf down dinner, then grab my bike.

"Chance!" Mom calls. "Be back before dark!"

It's only a ten-minute ride to Jordan's. In Austin in the summer, it doesn't get dark until at least 8:30. And it doesn't cool off until way, way after that. If ever. It's still plenty warm and humid right now—it feels like God has just taken a super-hot shower, opened the door, and let out all the steam.

I pedal faster, the breeze whipping against my face. It feels good. Ahead, there's a root pushed up through the sidewalk—the perfect ramp. I jump it, catch some air, then land and keep pedaling. It's not just the breeze that feels good, it's everything. Head Coach saying I had a good practice. Angela Savory smiling at me. And now going over to Jordan's, like usual. Like it's supposed to be. Maybe I can finally get Jordan to give me some advice about Angela, about—

I stop when I get to Jordan's. There's another bike in the driveway.

The bike's got a sticker on it that says BIG C. I don't have to be a rocket scientist to figure out who that stands for.

I thought Cole played at his own house?

For the first time, I realize Cole and I have names that start with the same letter. I'm not sure why that matters, but it does. *I'm* Jordan's C-friend, I say to myself. I was here first.

But then I realize how dumb that is. Everyone has friends whose names start with the same letter. If not, we'd each only have 26 friends. I laugh at myself.

Still, when I park my bike in the driveway, I wish it was the only one there. In my head, I picture a page from a CYOA book:

You see a strange bike in your best friend's driveway. Do you:

Take a pen and change the sticker to "Big

D," for Dummy? (Turn to p. 45)

Move the bike to someone else's driveway? (Turn to p. 57)

Turn around and ride home? (Turn to p. 14)

Go ring the doorbell? (Turn to p. 104)

I choose the last one.

"Yo, Chance-man!"

Jordan opens the door, punches my arm, then heads back inside. "Come on," he calls. "We're just setting up!"

In the living room, Cole is in the bean-bag chair. Where I usually sit.

"Hey, Peters," he says to me.

I nod at him and sit on the floor, my back against the couch. Jordan sprawls onto the rocker-recliner chair. He hands me a game console.

"You'll have to be on another team," Jordan says to me, pressing buttons on his console. "We can only do two people per team, on this version. I'm gonna get the multi-version soon."

"Okay," I say.

"So it'll be me and Cole," Jordan says, flipping

through selection screens, "and we'll find someone else online, to match you up with."

"I hope it's not that d-bag from Canada!" Cole says, laughing.

"Yeah," Jordan says. "Right, huh?"

Cole rolls his eyes. "Remember when he tried that stupid triple reverse, and we—"

"Creamed him!" Jordan yells, still flipping through screens. "Okay, cool," he says. "We got you teamed up with some dude in San Diego, so—" He glances down at his buzzing phone.

"Zee?" Cole asks.

"Yup," Jordan says.

He reaches for the phone, but Cole kicks it away.

"Hey," Jordan says, "what—"

"We're *playing*," Cole tells him. "No contact from the chicas while we play. I already told Jessica, she knows to leave me alone."

"Yeah," Jordan says, "but Zee…"

"Is a *girl*," Cole says. "She'll wait. Plus, girls like it when you play 'the game.' Trust me."

"The game?" I ask.

Cole turns to me. "Seriously, Peters? Don't you

know anything?"

Apparently not, I think. But I don't want to get Cole mad at me. Maybe he's going to tell me what everyone else knows, what I somehow missed this summer. I keep quiet.

"'The game,'" Cole continues, "is the cardinal rule of dating."

I lean forward. Now *this* is what I've been waiting for.

Cole counts off on his fingers. "First, love 'em." He leans toward me. "That means making out," he says, as if I'm in second grade.

I nod.

"Second, talk to 'em. Even if you don't like it, you gotta do that part."

I nod again.

"And third—and this is the key—ignore 'em."

"Ignore?" I say.

Cole smiles. "Yup. You give girls too much attention, they get smothered. So, you kiss 'em a bit. Talk to 'em a bit. Then ignore 'em a bit. Always works."

I turn to Jordan. "Is that what you do with Zee?"

"Well," Jordan says, "Zee…"

"Is a *girl*," Cole says again. He kicks Jordan's phone further across the floor. "Now, are we gonna play, or what?"

Jordan looks at his phone for a second. Is he going to tell Cole off?

But then he lets out a laugh and hits Cole in the arm. "Dude," Jordan says, "she's gonna kill me."

"Yeah," Cole tells him, "but she'll *love* you for it. Have I been wrong?"

Jordan shakes his head. "Not yet."

"Not ever," Cole says. "Now, let's dominate the football world!"

The two of them high five.

I wonder if Cole's been telling Jordan what to do with Zee, ever since football camp. And I wonder if I should try it—should I use "the game" with Angela?

Jordan hits the start button and hands me a controller.

"Press red to pass or kick," he tells me, "blue to hand off, green to jump, yellow to head fake, orange to tackle, and black to switch between players. Got it?"

"Um, kinda."

"You'll get the hang in no time."

We start playing, but I do not get the hang in no time. Or any time.

Jordan and Cole seem like they've been playing together for months (have they?), and they're killing me and the guy from San Diego. After the first quarter, it's 34 to 7. In the second quarter, the guy from San Diego logs off. Jordan hits pause.

Cole sets down his controller. "Wow, Peters. You're pretty sucky at games, huh?"

Only when the games are sucky, I think.

"Hey, we should get that Spielman quitter to play," Cole says. He laughs. "Maybe you could beat him, at least."

"Ha ha," I say.

"That guy is such a pansy," Cole says.

"He's not so—" I stop mid-sentence. What am I doing?

Cole tilts his head at me. "Peters? You're not friends with that quitter, are you?"

"Of course not," I say. I glance at Jordan. His brow is furrowed. Not like he's mad, more like he's confused. "So, uh, what other games do you have?" I ask him. Maybe there's a *World Baseball Domination* game.

Jordan shrugs. "A bunch of stuff."

"Yeah," Cole says, "but they're all pretty lame." He picks up his controller. "You can watch me and Jordan play," he says. "Maybe you'll figure it out that way."

Sometimes, people say things and pretend they're being helpful, but they're really taking a dig at you. I am 99.9% sure that's what Cole is doing right now.

"You could play on my brother's," Jordan says to me. "He won't be home 'til late. He's got a bunch of games, in his room."

The thought of sitting in Jordan's brother's room by myself, playing *Lethal Death Hero Punisher* or whatever he's got, while Cole and Jordan cheer each other in the living room, doesn't sound like my idea of a super-happy fun time.

"That's okay," I say, "I gotta get home anyway."

"Really?" Jordan asks.

"Yeah, uh, my mom's making dinner late." Why did I just lie to him?

Cole is already turned back to the game. "Cool. See you tomorrow in practice."

"Yeah," I say.

92

I get up. Jordan stays on the floor, next to Cole.

"All right," Jordan says. "See you later."

I pause for a second. I want to say something, but I have no idea what. Jordan and Cole are facing the screen, picking teams for a new game. I let myself out the front door.

Cole's bike is still in the driveway. I think about the CYOA choices I came up with earlier. I wonder if I picked the wrong one, by ringing the doorbell. I could still write on the sticker on Cole's bike. Or put it in someone else's driveway.

But instead, I get on my own bike, and ride home. It's not even close to being dark.

Space Club

The next morning the bus is full again. I see Angela way in the back. She's got her head down as usual, writing. She's sitting beside a red-haired girl.

"Take a seat, kid," the driver tells me. "We're late."

In the middle of the bus, I see Cole and cheerleader Jessica together, along with Zee and Jordan. Maybe this is the "sit with 'em" part of Cole's dating game.

Cole says something to Jordan, then makes a "loser" sign with one hand and points at Kevin. I fake a smile and roll my eyes, like I'm in on the joke, and sit beside Kevin.

Today Kevin's wearing a shirt with a collar and gray suspenders. He's holding a black binder with a piece of paper taped to it that says SPACE CLUB. A blue NASA sticker is in the bottom corner. He turns like he's about to say something to me, but a paper wad slams into his head with a whack!

"Kuh-kuh-kuh Quitter!" Cole yells out. I hear a few laughs.

The driver looks up in the rearview mirror. "Keep it down back there!"

Kevin pushes the ball of paper from his lap, onto the seat between us. I pick it up; the paper is wadded tight, hard. From the back, a low chant starts up, almost too quiet to hear.

"kuh … kuh … kuh …"

I know they're only chanting at Kevin, but for some reason it feels like they're talking to me, too. I wish Cole would just give it up.

"Kuh … Kuh … Kuh..."

The chant slowly gets louder, faster. And I can tell it's not just Cole. I wonder if Jordan is chanting with him. And Angela.

"Kuh, Kuh, Kuh …"

Don't they know that Kevin's new, that he doesn't know how everything works? I mean, nobody told him how big of a deal football was, did they?

"Kuh, Kuh, Kuh, *Quitter*!"

The bus erupts in laughter. For a split second I want to turn and hurl the paper wad like it's a baseball and bean stupid Cole right between the eyes. But of course I don't.

"Hey!" the driver calls. "I said keep it down!" His face is bright red. "Do not make me report this whole bus to the principal!"

The bus goes quiet; all I can hear are a few whispers. I wonder what they're saying. Are they talking about me, making fun of me, because I'm sitting with Kevin? Does everyone think we're friends? Does Angela? I drop the paper wad and take out my CYOA book.

"What's that?" Kevin asks.

I don't respond.

Behind us, the bus sounds go back to normal. I try to listen in on the conversations, but the bus engine is too loud, the words all blend together.

Kevin opens his black binder then closes it. "Do you like space stuff?" he asks.

I realize my CYOA book is titled *Space and Beyond*; I shut it and cram it in my backpack. All I want is to get to school, get to first period, get away from Kevin, and sit by Angela.

"I'm starting a Space Club," Kevin says. He's

holding his binder open. From the corner of my eye, I notice a fancy brochure with a picture of the space shuttle and a super close-up of the instrument panel, all covered with lights and touch screens and about fifty thousand different knobs and switches. I've never seen the controls in that much detail before.

"I'm thinking it can meet once a week," Kevin says, "right after school. We can talk about space stuff." He flips to another page in the binder. This one shows a picture of a blue and purple galaxy. "Did you know they found a new planet last week? It's in the next closest solar system, and it has twice as many rings as Saturn."

"They don't know for sure," I say. "The news said it's just a guess, that the rings might just be big gas clouds sticking out, or maybe—"

What am I doing? What if Jordan notices me chatting away with Kevin? What if Angela notices?

I take out my headphones.

"Yeah, I heard that, too," Kevin says, "but I still bet it's rings. Hey, you know what we could also do? A field trip to the UT observatory. Or to Houston, to NASA! They have some amazing telescopes. We learned about them this summer in space camp."

I untangle my headphone cords.

"So anyway," Kevin continues. "I was wondering. I thought maybe, you might want to be part of the Club." He closes the binder. "It needs at least two members to be official."

There's a burst of laughter from the back of the bus; I can only imagine what that's about.

I have to admit, the Space Club does sound kind of cool. But then, will everyone think I'm Kevin's best friend? I imagine the CYOA page:

The school dork just asked you to join his Space Club. Do you:

> *Say yes? (Turn to p. 65)*
> *Say no? (Turn to p. 19)*
> *Pretend to be deaf? (Turn to p. 92)*
> *Go sit in the bus driver's lap? (Turn to p. 39)*

I know it's harsh, but what else can I do? I've already got football after school. And even if it met at a different time, the whole bus would make fun of me. Just like they're already doing with Kevin.

"Sorry," I say, not looking over. I put my headphones on.

Spontaneity

Kevin doesn't look at me for the rest of the bus ride. In first period he takes his seat up front, his back to me, his back to everyone. I remind myself that, even if I did want to join his Space Club, I couldn't. I'd have to give up football. And there's absolutely, positively, 152% no way in the world I could do that. I'd be in the same boat as Kevin.

I picture the two of us in some leaky old dinghy, floating in the ocean, hundreds of miles from land. I read that's what pirates would do sometimes—capture a ship and put some of the crew in a tiny rowboat, with no oars or paddles or even food or water, then push them away from the main ship. The boat would just drift and drift and drift all alone, until everyone starved or went crazy or were eaten by sharks or maybe even by each other.

So really, I don't have a choice. But, staring at Kevin's back, I still kind of feel like crap.

"Good morning, Chance."

I'm lucky I'm not chewing gum, because I would've choked. As it is, I almost gag on the air itself. I forget all about pirate ships and Space Club and even football. Because Angela Savory just said Hi to me. And smiled. Again.

"Hangela," I say.

Which is not what I meant to come out. I'd planned for a separate and distinct "Hi," followed by a completely independent "Angela."

Hangela laughs. Was that funny? Maybe I should slur my words more often.

"I liked your essay," Angela says. She takes her mini notebook from her mini backpack. Today she's wearing dark jeans with white flip-flops, a yellow shirt with sleeves so short it's almost sleeveless, and earrings with feathers hanging down. The feathers remind me of a peacock, all shiny blacks and blues and greens. The green is the same shade as her eyes.

Wait—did she say she liked my essay?

"It was so, I don't know, *real*." Angela opens her notebook. "I wrote it down."

She's making fun of me, right? She wrote down what I said? The essay where I talked about "all the pretty colors"? The essay that was really about her?

I am so confused.

Angela hands me a tiny card, about the size of her pinky. Her fingernails are painted yellow, and each thumbnail has a green flower swirled in the center.

"Greenthumb," I say, pointing.

Oh my god, I sound like a little kid! Why don't I just point straight up and say "Whiteceiling!" Or point straight down and say "Browndesk!" Or at myself and say "Dumbchance!"

Angela grins. "Thanks for noticing." She stretches her thumbs out, which on some people might look like they were trying to hitch a ride, but on her it's incredibly cute. She puts the pinky-sized card on my desk. It has a tiny drawing of an angel with wings, dressed in a flowing yellow and white and green dress, leaping into the air, arms spread wide, laughing. The angel looks like a kid, trying to catch the sky. Beneath her, in cursive letters, it says *Spontaneity*.

Huh?

"It's a Life Card," Angela says. "I have a whole deck at home. Every morning I pick one, and it's my guiding word for the day. This is what I picked for today."

"Oh. Uh, cool."

Am I supposed to do something with the card? Something spontaneous?

I think for a second, then pick the card up and toss it in the air. "Wheee!" The card spins over and over, like a little propeller, then lands on the floor.

Angela looks at me like I just ate a baby dolphin.

"Chance?" At the front of the room, Ms. Fernandez is at the board. "If you're ready, I'd like to start class now."

Dating Advice

"So what was it?" Zee asks.

"Huh?"

We're at our lockers, just after first period. During which I did not say one (1) more word, after the Life Card incident.

"That little note Angela gave you," Zee says, trying to cram a book in her backpack. "The note you threw on the floor."

Great, did everyone see it? I spin the dial on my locker, but suddenly I can't remember the combination. "I didn't throw… It wasn't anything, just paper."

"Just paper?" Zee gives me her look, the head-tilt, I-know-more-than-you look.

I stop the dial at 12, even though it's not the right number, then switch directions and pretend I know what I'm doing. Zee keeps staring.

"Fine," I say. "It was something called a Life Card."

"Like the New Age stuff?"

I stop fake-spinning my locker dial. "Yeah, I think—wait, how do you know—"

"My mom's totally into all that," Zee says. "She buys chakra necklaces, love potions, Life Cards, the whole bit. She swears by it, but I think it's a load of donkey hockey."

Most kids cuss all the time, but Zee never does. She comes up with way more creative stuff.

Zee puts her backpack on the floor and steps on it, trying to get the zipper closed. It looks like she's got half the school library inside. "So," she asks, "what card did Angela give you?"

"It said 'Spontaneity.'"

"Ah, the Spontaneity card. That means she likes you."

"It does?"

"I have no idea," Zee says, smirking.

What? Why is she joking about this? Why am I even talking to her about Angela? I turn back to my locker.

"Sorry, Chance," Zee says, "I didn't mean to make fun." She touches my shoulder. For a flash, it reminds me of when Angela did the same thing, the first day of school. Zee pulls her hand away.

"But," she says, "maybe it really does mean that." Her voice doesn't sound like she's kidding now.

"Mean what?"

"That Angela wanted you to be spontaneous, and ask her out."

I turn the locker dial to some random numbers, replaying the start of first period in my head.

"But instead," I say, "I threw the card on the floor."

"And yelled out 'Wheee!'"

"Thanks for reminding me."

Zee lets out a big laugh. It's not big in an annoying, pack-of-rabid-hyenas way. It's more like what Mom would call "hearty." Which makes me think of pasta sauce. Which I like.

With one strong pull, Zee finally gets her backpack to come together. "Actually," she says, "it was pretty funny, tossing the card like that."

"It was?"

"Sure. To me, at least."

"So, do you really think…"

"What?" Zee cocks her head, like she's about give me her look again.

"That Angela wants me to ask her out?"

Zee swings her huge pack over her shoulders. "You know, *Chance*, let me give you some advice." She tugs on her straps and it makes her stoop forward a bit, like a hunchback. "Sometimes, you just have to take a chance."

"Huh?"

"Ask her out, dummy."

Oh.

The bell rings and Zee heads down the hall. "And Chance? You might want to think about writing down your locker combo."

Moon Landing

All I can think about for the rest of the morning is: should I ask Angela Savory out? Is that really what she meant by the card? I mean, she smiled at me, so that means something, right? Plus she totally liked my essay. So that's a lot of evidence in my favor. On the flip side, she could say no, or it could end up like my brain-strangle phone call. And then on the third side, or however many sides there are, maybe I should play Cole's "game" and ignore her for a while. Would that really work? What if someone else asks her out today, and then she has a boyfriend tomorrow? No, I need to ask her out first. Then, if she says yes, I can think about Cole and his "game."

Okay, if I'm going to ask Angela out, I need a good plan, I need—

My thoughts are cut short when I walk in the cafeteria for lunch. All along one wall, there are tables for different clubs, trying to recruit students. There's the Drama Club, the Spanish Club, and Student Council. At

108

the far end, there's a table covered in a white cloth and a small pile of charcoal briquettes labeled MOON ROCKS. The sign on the front of the table, in big blue letters, says JOIN SPACE CLUB!

And behind the table, of course, is Kevin Spielman. He's wearing the puffy silver metallic jacket from the first day, and has two white pillows attached to the back of it, like a rocket pack.

I see Jordan, sitting with Cole in the middle of the cafeteria, whispering to each other and shaking their heads at him.

What the heck is Kevin thinking? First he quits football, and now he's making an absolute dork of himself in front of the whole school, not just the football team. At this rate, he's going to be the most unpopular kid in the entire history of middle school.

Suddenly Kevin is up on the table, megaphone in his hand.

"Houston, the Eagle has landed! I repeat, the Eagle has landed!"

What the?

Kevin stretches one leg high and then puts it down, slowly, inch by inch, on the table, like he's walking in water. Or outer space.

I don't believe it—is he trying to re-create Apollo 11, the first moon landing?

A bunch of kids are watching. A few are quiet, like they might actually be interested, but most are pointing and laughing. I look around, but don't see Angela. Zee is sitting by Jordan, a smile on her face like she thinks it's funny, but not in a mean way.

"That's one small step for man," Kevin says into the megaphone, "and one giant leap for mankind!" He takes another big step, then plants a small American flag on the top of the table.

Oh, man.

Kevin straightens up and raises the megaphone.

"Just like Neil Armstrong was first on the moon, join the first-ever Space Club! We'll talk about the latest discoveries! We'll exchange space stories! We'll even try to go on field trips, maybe to—whoa!"

The megaphone flies into the air and Kevin does a little flip, landing flat on his back—or rather on the pillows he attached as his jet pack. The whole cafeteria is laughing now.

Beside the table, Cole lets go of the tablecloth he

just yanked. He sneaks off, and Jordan joins him. But before they make it to the door, Head Coach, the lunch monitor, grabs them.

I walk over to the table. Slowly, Kevin rolls onto his side, then steps down.

"Are you okay?" I ask.

Kevin adjusts his glasses. "Sure, I'm fine. The pillows broke my fall." He picks up the flag and some of the charcoal briquettes on the floor. I start to help, then realize the whole school is probably watching. What the heck am I doing?

I turn and head toward the lunch line, without saying another word.

*   *   *

In football, Head Coach makes Jordan and Cole run laps the entire practice, as punishment for the cafeteria incident. And it's weird—I'm of course happy that Cole is getting punished, but I have to admit, I'm also a little happy that Jordan is, too. Why? Cole was the only one who pulled out the tablecloth. Shouldn't I be siding with my best friend?

I'm still trying to figure it all out when Head Coach lights into me.

"*Peters!* What's wrong with you today? You're supposed to hit the *right* side of the line. You do know your right from left, don't you?"

After that we run a bunch of new plays, including a pretty cool pass to me, all the way out to the sideline. But I can't seem to get my heart into it.

Why not? I mean, it's not like I love getting pounded by the defense every time I get the ball, but it's also not the end of the world. I don't feel like this with baseball, do I?

In baseball, things are more connected. Like when I'm playing outfield and someone hits a line drive to the corner and I sprint as fast as I can, diving at the last minute and the ball goes just past my glove, but I land in a kind of somersault and spring up, find the ball where it's bounced off the fence, grab it in one swoop (in my bare hand, not the glove), take three quick steps and find my cut-off man at the same time, rear back and zip the ball to the infield, where the cut-off man catches it, turns on a dime, and fires the ball to third as the runner is sliding into the red dirt, and the third baseman catches the ball and sweeps his glove at the same time, barely tagging the runner out.

But football is different.

Most of football is about running into people or pushing them around. Sure, there are times when I break free and get to sprint a few yards, maybe even all the way to the endzone if I'm lucky (or not listening to Head Coach). But most of the time I'm smashing into other guys, trying to move them a few yards this way, a few yards that way. It's pretty much like lifting weights. Which is not my—

"Peters!"

Head Coach's voice sears across the field. I realize I'm standing on the sideline, the entire offense waiting for me to come back to the huddle. I clutch the ball and sprint over.

*   *   *

Mom's waiting at the curb after practice, like normal. I hop in the car, my whole body sore, and lean the seat way back.

"Rough practice today?"

I start to tell her it's not just today's practice. But Mom's never played sports, much less football, so there's no way she would understand. If Dad were here, he'd probably just tell me to suck it up.

"It wasn't too bad," I say, closing my eyes.

"I see."

The car engine hums, and I can feel the seat vibrating beneath me. It's amazing how much more you notice with your eyes closed.

"So," Mom says, "how about the rest of the day? Do anything interesting?"

"No, not really." I think back to first period, to Angela giving me her Life Card, me throwing it on the floor. And Zee telling me I should ask her out. Should I?

"I was thinking burgers for dinner," Mom says. "How's that sound?"

"Great."

Maybe I should call Angela tonight. But what would I say?

"Hi, Angela. Do you want to go out?"

"Sure, Chance, I'd love to! Where?"

"Uhhh..."

Okay, that's not going to work. I need to figure out where I could take her. Maybe Mom knows some good places. Should I ask her? I slide one eye open. She's leaning forward, checking her teeth in the rearview mirror, lips stretched back like a crazy clown.

Um, no.

At home I spend an hour online, but nothing good comes up. I make a list of some restaurants, but none seem quite right. Also on the list is the high school play, *My Fair Lady* (which sounds kind of lame, and isn't for another month), watching the bats at the Congress Street bridge (not bad, but too touristy), a robotics exhibit at the Children's Museum (cool, but more for little kids), and about a gazillion different bands playing downtown (very cool, but those places all are 18 and up). I even skim my CYOA, searching for endings that might have a kid who saves the universe by taking a girl on the perfect date. There aren't any.

How am I supposed to figure this out? How do other kids figure out where to go? Do I even *know* other guys who go out with girls?

Duh—of course I do! I pick up my phone to call Jordan, then stop. Isn't he just going to tell me to play Cole's "game"? Or maybe he'll tell me to talk to Cole, which of course is out of the question. No, for whatever reason, it doesn't feel right, calling Jordan, asking him for advice. For whatever reason, I just don't want to.

But I need to do something…

I try to put myself in Jordan's head, figure out where he would go on a date. But all I can think of is Jordan talking about football. That, and playing video games. With Cole. He likes other stuff, doesn't he?

Of course he does. And he and Zee must have gone out tons of times. Heck, with Jordan's older brother giving them rides, I bet they've been to every cool place in town together.

Together. The two of them.

Of course—I don't have to call Jordan at all.

*   *   *

"Hello?"

"Hi. Um, is Zee there?"

"Can I tell her who's calling?"

For a second I want to say, "I don't know, *can you?*" but I keep that to myself.

"Um, it's Chance. Chance Peters."

"Oh! Hi, Chance! We haven't seen you in ages! How's your mother doing?"

I forget that Zee's mom and my mom used to hang out, back when we were in first and second grade. They used to make Zee and me play together. But that was

116

forever ago.

"Um, she's good, great. Still a dentist."

Still a dentist? How dorky does that sound?

"That's good. Well, it's great to hear your voice,
Chance." She pauses. "Zee!"

I have to hold the phone back a bit; Zee's mom
apparently doesn't believe in covering the phone when
she yells.

A couple seconds later, Zee picks up.

"Hello?"

"Hey, Zee."

"Who's this?"

"It's me. Chance."

"Well well well. And what do I owe this honor to,
the great Chance Peters calling little old me?"

What is she talking about?

"What I mean," Zee says, as if she can read my
mind, "is that you pretty much haven't called me since
fifth grade."

"I—we talk in school," I say.

"No, *I* talk to *you* in school. You just react."

I try to think if that's true. I'm not sure.

"So anyway," Zee says, "like I was saying,

what are you calling for? Did you forget your locker combination again?"

Suddenly asking Zee doesn't seem like such a great idea.

"I, uh…"

"Yes?"

At least Zee knows about Angela—she's the one who told me to ask her out in the first place. And I've really got nowhere else to turn.

"I'm thinking," I say, "about asking Angela out."

"Thinking about it?"

"Okay, well, I'm *planning* to do it."

"You called to tell me that?"

"No. Well, yes. That, and that I'm … I'm having a hard time figuring out where to take her."

The last part comes out in a tumble of words; it's surprisingly hard to say.

"Zee?"

There's no response. What—did she hang up?

"Zee? Hello?"

"Yeah yeah yeah, just a second loverboy, I'm thinking."

She's thinking? About what? About whether to

laugh? Tell Jordan? Tell me off?

"Okay," Zee says, "I think I can help."

"Really?"

"No, I like to make things up." Zee pauses. "Sorry, that's just one of my pet peeves, when people say *'Really?'* It's like they think I'm lying, like all they have to do is say 'Really?' and I'll turn around say, 'Oh oh, you got me! Okay, here's the *real* truth!' Man, that really gets me."

I want to tell her one of my pet peeves is when people drag out telling me something super-important, like how they think they can help me ask out Angela Savory.

But all I say is: "Um, yeah. I've never thought about it like that."

"Okay, Chance, here it is: You should ask Angela on a double-date. With me and Jordan."

"Re—"

I catch the "Really?" before it's all the way out.

"—ally good idea," I add quickly.

But is it a good idea? Really?

"Yes," Zee says, "it's a great idea. Jordan may not love it, but that's his problem."

Jordan may not love it? Why not?

But I decide to leave that for another time. Right now there are more important things to ask Zee.

"So," I say, "where are we going?"

Asking Out Angela

I hang up the phone after talking to Zee for a few more minutes. It turns out she and Jordan already have something planned, for Saturday. Jordan's brother is taking them to Home Slice Pizza for dinner. And now, Angela and I are going with them.

As soon as I ask her.

"Chance?" It's Mom, outside my bedroom door. "The burgers are almost ready."

"Okay, I'll be there in a sec."

Mom walks off. It's 7:15 p.m. By the time we're done eating and finished with the dishes, it might be too late to call. And tomorrow is Friday. I can't ask Angela out just one day before, can I? No, even with no girlfriend experience at all, I know that's a bad idea.

I pick up the phone and dial her number.

"Hello?"

"Um, hi, is Angela there?"

"This is Angela."

Great—nice job, Chance. Way to recognize her

voice.

"Oh, hi Angela! This is Chance!"

Why am I yelling?

"Hey, Chance." She sounds happy. Like she's smiling. ☺

Okay, now what? I really should have written this out.

"So," I say. "Um, what are you up to?"

"We just finished dinner. I'm about to start our English homework."

"Oh yeah. Cool. Me too."

What am I saying? We're about to *start* dinner, and I haven't even thought about our English homework.

"That's neat," Angela says.

"Yeah…"

Come on, Chance, just say something! Anything!

"So," I say, "I was wondering…"

Why did I stop? I force my mouth back open, my tongue to move.

"I was wondering … if maybe, if you weren't doing anything Saturday night…"

I wait for Angela to react, but there's only silence.

"I was wondering if maybe … you'd want to go

get some pizza. With me. And Zee and Jordan."

"Sure! That sounds great!"

"Really?" I could kick myself for saying that.

"Of course! I have to ask my parents, but I'm sure they'll say it's okay."

I feel like an entire planet has been lifted off my back and I'm light as air, light as oxygen itself, like I can zip around the room, like I can actually fly.

I am going out with Angela Savory!

*   *   *

"Well, you sure look happy."

Mom slides me a plate with a burger on it, and some salad.

"Mmm-hmm," I say, taking a huge bite. It's the best burger I've ever tasted. "These are awesome."

"Why thank you, Chance. But please don't talk with your mouth full."

I nod and swallow. "Sorry."

"So, are you happy about football?"

"Nope." I take a big drink of milk. "I'm going on a date!"

As soon as I say it, I realize I've made a mistake. Mom and I have never talked about girls, I've avoided it like yellow fever, but that's just changed.

"A date?"

I nod. "Uh-huh. A double-date, actually. With Jordan, and Zee."

"I see. And who is the girl you're taking?"

Oh great, now we have to have full-out conversation about it.

I take a breath. Okay. If I can ask out Angela on the phone, I can talk to Mom about this. "Her name is Angela. She just moved here from Tennessee."

"She's in your class?"

"Yeah."

"Well." Mom leans back. "And when is this date scheduled?"

"Um, for Saturday. We're going to get pizza. At Home Slice."

"Is that so?" Mom raises an eyebrow.

Wait—is she going to say I can't go? Oh no no no, please no. That would absolutely, positively, totally, completely, obliterate my life.

Mom rests her chin on her hands, looks at me. "And when, Chance, where you planning to ask my permission for all this?"

124

"I..."

"Were you just going to tell me as you were heading out the door on Saturday?" Mom doesn't give me a chance to answer. "And not only that," she continues, "but how exactly do the four of you plan on getting to the pizza place?"

"Jordan's brother. Randy. He's, uh, he's going to drive." I realize I'm still holding my half-eaten burger in my hand. It feels cold, hard. I set it on the plate. "I … I'm sorry, Mom. I should have asked. I just … I just got too excited, I guess."

Mom is still staring at me, chin in her hands.

I exhale, slowly, and sit up in my chair. "So," I say. "Um, can I have permission? To go on a date?"

"Thank you, Chance, for asking."

Mom doesn't say anything more, she just sits there, staring at me.

Come on, say something! Come *on*!

Finally she sighs, then smiles big. "Yes," she says, "you can go."

Date Prep

After dinner, I help Mom with the dishes, then go to my computer. I look up the menu for Home Slice and memorize every choice, then read all the online reviews I can find, so I can know exactly what to recommend to Angela. The "Meatball Moonwalk" pizza has the top ratings: *Mountains of meatballs, smothered in layers of cheese as smooth as the moonwalk. It's like heaven in your mouth.* And one review even tells exactly where to sit: *The tables by the front window are the best! You can watch people walk by and it gives you tons to talk about—perfect for a date!*

Perfect!

After that I make lists of stuff to talk about during dinner, conversation topics. I cut-and-paste the jokes from my original List, the one I used when I first called Angela. I also copy some of the info I found about Memphis and Tennessee. But what else? Baseball? Football? Is Angela even into sports? I add that to my list of PQs (Potential Questions): "PQ #3: So, do you

126

like sports?"

What else does she like?

I think back to when she smiled at me, and said she liked my essay. I pull out the crumpled, handwritten page. It's all about colors, but also mentions vanilla ice cream, suit buttons, and kites. I do some research on all those topics and find a few good things, including the Zilker Kite Festival they have in the park every spring. Maybe Angela is totally into kites. I find a ton of stuff about them online—plenty to make it through dinner. Finally I do some research on Life Cards and find out they are a whole set of cards, each with one word that's supposed to guide you through the day, like *Trust* or *Vision* or *Transformation*.

I hit print then flop into bed, dreaming of Angela and pizza and meatballs on the moon.

*   *   *

The next day, Friday, I see Angela as soon as I walk on the bus. She's in the back, sitting next to the red-haired girl again. For a second, I'm disappointed. Why didn't she save a seat for me? But then I realize I might have to use up a bunch of the topics I mapped out for dinner. I definitely want to save those—I don't want to waste all my best conversation before tomorrow night.

I wave at Angela and she waves back. And, from the middle of the bus, so does Zee.

Even though I wasn't waving at her, I give Zee a little half-wave, too. Jordan is sitting beside her. He glances back at Angela, then turns and furrows his brow, but this time it looks more like he's mad than confused. What? Does he still want to hit on Angela Savory? Across the aisle from him, Cole is shaking his head at me, like I've just fumbled the football. What did I do to him?

I really wish I understood people better.

"Kid," the driver tells me, "we can't go anywhere until you *sit*. Make a choice."

I plop into my usual seat up front, next to Kevin. He's reading a book about black holes. I get out the list I made last night, going over it again.

"Home Slice is awesome."

I look up and see Kevin, peering over.

"You've been there?" I ask.

Kevin nods. "My parents took me in the summer, right after we moved. I had the Pirate's Booty pizza, where they put rounded pieces of pineapple on top, like a pile of gold coins."

That actually sounds kind of cool. Should I order the Pirate's Booty pizza instead of the Meatball Moonwalk?

"It was delicious," Kevin says. He glances at my lists. "I've never been there on a date, though. Actually, I've never been on a date at all."

I'm about to tell him I haven't either, but decide to keep that to myself.

"My mom and dad go on dates all the time," Kevin tells me.

I'm not sure I want to hear about Kevin's parents going out together.

"Oh," is all I say.

"Mostly they just do regular stuff, you know?"

No, I don't know.

"Like skipping rocks," Kevin says.

"Huh?"

"Last week they went to Town Lake. Then they stood at the shore and threw rocks across the water, seeing who could skip the farthest."

"That's it?"

"Yup. My dad says that's the best way to get to know someone. Just standing there, skipping rocks together."

For a second, I picture taking Angela Savory to Town Lake, throwing rocks out across the water together. I do have a good arm. A great arm, actually. But then I think about inviting her:

"So, Angela?"

"Yes, Chance?"

"About tomorrow."

"Oh, yes, I'm so excited! I love pizza!!"

"Yeah, me too. But I was thinking, instead..."

"Is there something even better? What is it, what is it?"

"Well, I was thinking we could, um ... that we could go to the lake, and..."

"Oooo, and what!?"

"And skip rocks."

I look at Kevin. He's wearing a long-sleeved shirt with practically every color in it, all jumbled together in different shapes and sizes, like he accidentally washed it with a box of open magic markers.

This is the guy who quit football. This is the guy who tried to re-enact the first moon landing to get people in his Space Club. This is the guy who just moved here, who's never been out with a girl, who doesn't have a single friend. Why in the world would I take his advice?

"Thanks," I say, "but I think I'll stick with pizza."

*   *   *

In first period, Angela is wearing a peach-colored dress and brown flip-flops. She looks awesome.

"Hi, Chance," she says.

"Hey."

"I'm so excited about tomorrow!"

"Yeah, me too."

She leans forward in her desk, like she's waiting for me to say something.

I check the clock. There's still five minutes before class starts.

"I, uh … you like pizza?" I ask.

What kind of question is that?

Before Angela can answer, there's a shot to my left arm.

Fact-check: Sometimes I really, really don't like it when Jordan does that.

"Dude," Jordan says, "it's a little late to ask her that, isn't it?"

Angela giggles.

Zee walks up, leans on the desk behind Angela's. "So, Chance, what're you wearing tomorrow night?"

"Oh, I'm sure he's had that planned out for weeks," Jordan says.

Angela giggles again. Why is that so funny? I only asked her on the date yesterday, so there's no way I could have—

"Just kidding, Chance-man!" Jordan must have caught the look on my face. What was it? Did I look angry? Confused? Scared?

"If you want," Jordan says, "you can borrow my tie."

I feel my shoulders relax a bit. This is the Jordan I know. I wonder why he's being himself again. Is it because he's trying to impress Zee? Or Angela? Or … and then I realize, Cole's not in our first period class. Here, Jordan is being Jordan-Jordan, not Cole-Jordan.

"Thanks," I tell him, "but I think … I'll figure something out."

"I think you should wear blue," Zee says. "It brings out your eyes."

I feel my face go hot. What's she doing?

Jordan huffs at her.

"What?" Zee asks. "I'm only giving him some advice."

"Yeah," Jordan says, "but…"

But you're doing it right in front of my date, I think.

Jordan shakes his head at her. He understands. And, thankfully, he's helping me out again. If Zee had said that, with just me and Angela here…

Angela is glancing from Jordan to Zee. She seems confused.

"Whatever," Zee says. "Chance, I was just trying to help." She goes back to her seat.

Angela looks over at me. I look over at her. What do I say now?

I check the clock again. Still three minutes to class. Maybe Ms. Fernandez will start early…

"Yes," Angela says to me.

"What?"

"Yes," Angela repeats, "I like pizza."

"Oh. Good."

I try to think of something else to say, but my head's an empty barrel. Maybe I should break out the list for tomorrow night. It wouldn't hurt to use up just one question, right? I'm about to ask Angela if she like sports, but she speaks first.

"Do you?" she asks.

"Do I what?"

"Like pizza?"

"Um, yeah. Pizza's great."

Angela nods. "It is."

Two minutes left.

Behind me, I swear I can hear someone laughing under their breath.

I check my fingers. How did my nails get so long already? I need to remember to trim them, before the date tomorrow. I put my hands under my legs.

Angela watches me, like she's waiting to talk.

"So," I say.

Angela leans forward. One minute until class.

"So, um, so I'll see you tomorrow?" I ask.

Angela nods. "Yes."

"Great."

Thirty seconds left.

"I'm looking forward to it," I say.

"Me too!"

Finally Ms. Fernandez starts class. I'm worried

that Angela thinks I'm as boring as floor tile, but halfway through class she catches my eye and smiles again. I'm on cloud nine. No, cloud ten, eleven and twelve. So what if we didn't have the best conversation a little while ago? This is English class, you're not supposed to be chatting away. I think of the list I've made for tomorrow night and feel 120% better. Tomorrow, we'll have plenty of stuff to talk about. Good, interesting, funny, date-perfect stuff.

The rest of the day pretty much flies by. In football, I screw up a bunch, and Head Coach chews me out, but for once I don't really care. I've crossed off the number one item on my Main To-Do List.

I, Chance Allen Peters, have a girlfriend.

Double Date

The next morning is Saturday. Date Day.

I'm up early, double flossing and brushing my teeth, washing my hair an extra five minutes. Mom takes me shopping, all the way to the outlet mall. She seems even more excited than I am about finding the perfect outfit. At one store, Mom holds up a white button-down with multi-colored stripes. It's like someone took a 64-crayon box and decided to draw a line with each one. It also reminds me of something else. I laugh.

"What?" Mom says.

"Nothing, it's just … this kid at school has a shirt kind of like that."

"What kid?"

"Oh, just this new kid, Kevin."

Mom twirls around, the shirt sleeves lagging just behind her, like little wings. "Well, I think this Kevin has wonderful taste." She shoots me a mock smile.

"Maybe you should pick out *his* clothes," I say,

joking.

Mom finds a few more of the worst-looking shirts in the history of clothing, but we do end up finding one that looks pretty good on me: a navy Polo, with a little front pocket. I realize it's a blue shirt. Just like Zee said.

Mom and I stop for lunch at the food court, but I only eat half my chicken sandwich—I don't want to ruin my appetite for tonight.

"So," Mom says, swallowing a bite of moo-shoo pork. "Tell me about this girl."

Ugh. Do we have to?

"I already did," I say. "Her name's Angela, she moved here from Tennessee."

Mom takes out her small case of toothpicks. "Well, why do you like her, Chance?"

Because she's hot, I think to myself. Because she's the perfect girlfriend. Because she smiled at me and her eyes are the kind of green that would launch a million ships, and not those old-time sailing ships but hyper-warp spaceships that would cross the entire universe, and because she liked my essay.

"Um, she's nice," I say.

Mom shakes out a toothpick for herself, hands one

to me.

"I hope so," she says.

What am I supposed to say to that? See, this is why I don't talk to Mom about stuff like girls. I wonder what Dad would be saying, if he were here. Would he give me some tips on what to do on the date? Or just ask me about football? Maybe he could give me some tips on that, too. Or at least tell me that the games are worth all the practices. And heck, he's dating someone right now, isn't he? That woman I heard on the voicemail? Mom hasn't been out with anyone in years.

"Mom?"

She takes the toothpick from her teeth. "Mmm-hm?"

"Do you … do you have Dad's number?"

The toothpick dips in her hand. I didn't realize a toothpick could look sad.

"Chance, I'm not sure if…" She trails off. Then she puts the toothpick in her trash pile. "Yes. I have his number." She takes out her purse and writes it down for me.

"Thanks."

Mom pulls out her floss dispenser, tears off a long

piece, and hands it to me.

"Chance? Just—just don't expect too much, okay?"

"Yeah, okay." I take the piece of floss. Mom watches, to make sure I get every spot.

*   *   *

When we get home, I've only got twenty minutes before Jordan's brother is coming over to pick me up. I cut the tag off my new shirt, put on my best jeans and sneakers, and plant myself in front of the mirror.

The Polo shirt fits almost perfectly (it's the most expensive shirt Mom's ever bought me), and the navy blue actually does kind of match my eyes. Thanks, Zee.

My hair is poofy as always, but nothing I can do about that, other than shaving it all off or wetting it down with gel. Neither of those seems like a good idea. My face is a little sunburned (I forgot to put on sunscreen this morning), but it's nothing to worry about. All in all, I don't look half bad.

You have five minutes before being picked up for your first-ever date. Do you:

Try and call your Dad for advice?
(Turn to p. 56)

Ask Mom for any last-minute tips?
(Turn to p. 57)

Look up "world's best first-dates"
online? (Turn to p. 58)

Drink a Coke? (Turn to p. 12)

I decide to change the rules a bit, and do both of the last two choices. I grab a Coke from the fridge and do some searches for How to Succeed on Your First Date.

Five minutes later, Jordan's brother, Randy, pulls up to our house. Right on time.

"Yo, Chance-man!" Randy leans out the window of his 4-Runner. He's like a bigger version of Jordan with shaggy hair. They even sound the same. "Ready for some fun times at the pizza house?" he asks.

Mom walks out with me. Thankfully, Angela's not in the car—it's only Jordan and Zee, in the back seats. Zee has on jeans and a bright red tank top. Jordan is wearing the same outfit he wore the first day of school, arms crossed. I think about what Zee said on the phone, about him not being happy with the double-date idea.

Should I say something to him? What? "Hey, Jordan, is it okay if Angela and I come too?" It's a bit late for that. Suddenly I'm nervous, which is really,

really weird. Why should I be nervous about hanging out with Jordan? If anything, I should be nervous about Angela. Well, I'm sure I will be, once we get to her house.

"We're picking up Chance's hot date last," Randy says, grinning at me and Mom.

Mom puts on her dentist voice, the one that says, *If you don't behave, I'm about to drill into your root canal.*

"Randy," she says.

His smile fades.

"Randy, I expect you to take extra good care of Chance, of everyone in this car, all of whom are now your responsibility. I've known you for a long time. Don't let me down."

"Um, no. No, ma'am."

"Thank you, Randy. I'll expect Chance back here by 8:00 p.m. Sharp."

"Yes, ma'am. Of course."

I get in the front seat and roll my eyes at Randy, to say I'm sorry. He winks at me and we pull away, Mom waving from the driveway.

"Damn, Rand-man!" Jordan calls from the back

seat. "She practically has you on leash!"

Zee groans. "Jordan, you said the same thing about me and your tie, the first day of school. Are you ever going to use a *different* joke?"

"I could," Jordan says. "But that one always kills!"

"Maybe to you," Zee says.

Randy nudges me. "So, Chance-man, excited about your date? Nervous? Ready to puke?"

I laugh. "Yeah. A little of each."

"Good." Randy glances at my clothes. "Nice outfit, my man."

"Thanks."

"I think you look nice, too," Zee says from the back.

I turn around. "Really?" I say it with a little extra emphasis, to let her know I'm joking.

Zee grins and hits me, lightly, on the arm. As she leans back I can smell her shampoo; it smells like strawberries, my all-time favorite ice cream flavor. And I realize her red shirt kind of matches the way she smells. Do girls plan stuff like that?

"Oooo, me too, Chancey!" Jordan mocks. "I

142

think you look gorrrrgeous!"

I know he's just trying to be funny, but for some reason it reminds me of Cole. Jordan shoots a punch at me but I dodge—for once, I saw it coming. I wonder why I haven't been able to do that before.

"So, Mr. Style," Randy says to me. "Where to?"

Suddenly my stomach falls straight down, out of my body, through the floor of the car, and onto the street below. I swear I feel a bump as the back tires of Randy's 4-Runner drive over it. We keep moving. Somewhere, back on the asphalt, my flattened stomach is lying in the middle of the road.

"I, uh…"

How, how, HOW could I not have remembered to get Angela's address?

I spent the last two days researching our date, the last five minutes even, getting tips online. But I never thought about actually *getting* there.

"Dude," Jordan says, "don't you know where she lives?"

"I, urm…"

Randy chuckles. For a second, I think he's making fun of me. "Don't sweat it, Chance-man," he says. "Same thing happened to me, on my first date!"

"It did?"

"You bet."

"What did you do?"

"You've got her number, right? Just call her."

Of course. I take out my cell phone. "Thanks, Randy."

He gives me a little salute. "No prob."

I dial Angela's number. It rings. And rings. And then goes to voicemail. I hang up and try again. And again. Then I text her. There's no response.

Oh. Crap.

"Umm…"

Randy pulls the car to the curb, parks.

In the back seat, Jordan is cracking up. "This is awesome," he says.

"Jordan Vargas." Zee hits his shoulder. "It is *not* awesome."

What the heck am I supposed to do now? My first date with Angela Savory—with anyone—and it's going to end before it even begins. I still have the slip of paper with Dad's number on it, in my wallet. What would he say?

144

"Don't worry about it, Mr. High School! You should be out practicing football anyway!"

Why didn't I ask Angela where she lived? Or at least try and look up her address when I was online? If only Mom let me have Internet on my phone, I could try to find it now. But she says I'm too young…

"Randy?" I ask.

"Chance-man?"

"Does your phone have Internet?"

"Of course. Why—oh, good thinking!"

Randy gets out his phone, I tell him Angela's name, he punches it in. There are two listings for Savory in our neighborhood. It's almost like a CYOA: *Do you pick address #1 or #2?* I tell Randy to go to the first one, since it's closest to our bus route.

We pull up to the house. It's one-story, red brick mixed with tan wood panels. There are no cars parked in the driveway or out front. The yard is a mix of brown and green grass. The green part needs to be mowed.

"Well?" Randy says.

I'm still sitting in the front seat. What if this isn't the right house? Or what if her parents answer and don't like me? Or what if—

"Chance," Zee says from the back. "Just go ring the bell, it won't kill you."

I do a quick half-laugh, then get out. It's humid and the five-thirty sun is beating on my forehead, temples and neck. I can feel the sweat beads pushing out of my pores. All of them. I wipe my forehead and head up the front path. Part of me hopes this isn't Angela's house, so she doesn't see me dripping sweat down my—

"Hi, Chance!"

Angela's door flies open, and she skips down the steps. She's wearing a light green dress, the exact same color as her eyes, and brown heels. She looks amazing.

"Hi," I say. "You look amazing."

Angela smiles. "Thanks."

I glance around. "Aren't you parents here?"

Angela shakes her head. "They're both at work."

"Oh, okay."

And then, just like I read about online, I offer Angela my elbow. She giggles and puts her arm in mine. Suddenly, it's like the sweat has vaporized from my skin, and I'm dry as a desert, cool as an ice cube, steady as a … well, something that's really really steady. I'm as steady as me!

We walk back to Randy's car, arm-in-arm. I feel like I'm escorting the queen herself to the royal ball. Me, Chance Allen Peters! On a date! With Angela Savory!

As I walk by Randy's window, he let out a low whistle. "Damn, Chance-man, you know how to pick 'em!"

I open the front door for Angela, just like I read about, then close it after she's in her seat. Then I race to the back door and get in beside Zee and Jordan. Zee's in the middle, right beside me. She pats my leg, grinning. Jordan's giving me a scowl.

What? I mouth to him. But he just shakes his head.

"All right kids," Randy says, "let's get you guys some pizza!"

Randy drops us off and we get a table by the front window, just like I wanted.

"So," Jordan says, "you wanna get one big pizza and share? Cole told me the Pirate's Booty is awesome."

"Yeah, that's what Kevin said, too."

Jordan looks at me like I've grown a third nostril. "Dude, are you like best buds with that loser, or what?"

"No, I just … he was just babbling about it on the

bus the other day. I don't…"

Jordan closes his menu. "Well, Cole says it's the best, so we're getting Pirate's Booty."

"Um, hello?" Zee says. "Do *I* get a say in this?"

"Oh," Jordan says. "I, well…"

"Not *every*one likes the same thing," Zee says.

Jordan opens his menu again.

Zee turns to me and Angela. "Like with ice cream," she tells us.

I'm not really sure what she's talking about.

"Jordan loves chocolate," Zee continues, "my fave is peach, other people like vanilla or whatever, and it's all good." She pauses. "Except people who like coffee-flavored. Those people? Those people are just plain wrong."

Angela and I both laugh. Sometimes, Zee can be pretty cool.

Zee gives me a quick wink, then nods in Angela's direction. It takes me a second to realize what she's trying to tell me.

I turn to Angela. "So, what sounds good to you?" I ask. "We can get whatever you want, but the Meatball Moonwalk is supposed to be awesome. Like heaven in your mouth."

"Really?"

Beside me, Zee lets out a tiny snort.

"Yeah," I say, kicking Zee under the table. "Really."

We end up ordering a small Moonwalk, Jordan and Zee get a small Pirate's Booty. While we wait, the waitress brings us all Cokes. Angela stirs hers with her straw for a bit, before drinking it. Jordan's got his arms crossed, looking at the other tables. What's his deal? Then I realize—maybe this is part of the "game" Cole was talking about. Maybe this is the "ignore 'em" part. Should I do that too, with Angela?

Zee kicks my foot under the table, then motions with her head at Angela. Angela is staring at a photo of grapes on the wall.

You are sitting in a restaurant with your date. Do you:

> *Ignore her? (Turn to p. 1)*
>
> *Talk to her? (Turn to p. 12)*
>
> *Take a huge gulp of Coke and start a burping contest? (Turn to p. 39)*

"So," I say to Angela, "do you like sports?"

"Hmm? Sports? Yeah, I think so. Sure."

"Me too. I love sports. What's your favorite?"

"My dad watches golf."

Golf? I don't know a thing about golf.

"I love golf," I say.

"Actually," she says, "I don't know much about it."

"Oh."

Strike one on the sports topic.

I mentally scan my list of other conversation starters. "You know what's really cool?" I say. "Kites. There's a huge kite festival here every spring, in Zilker Park."

Angela takes a long sip of Coke. "Kites?"

"Yeah, you know. Like the ones you fly. Like in my essay."

"Oh yeah. I really liked that essay."

"Thanks."

I wait for Angela to speak, but she's looking at me like I'm the one who's supposed to say something. The waitress comes and refills our drinks.

"I gotta go to the bathroom," Jordan says. He gets up and heads to the back of the restaurant.

Zee stands. "Yeah, me too."

The two of them walk off. Is that some kind of secret code? Are you supposed to go to the bathroom together, on a date? Maybe they're going back there to make out. That's the second part of "the game" from Cole: "love 'em." Well, at least that means when they get back, Jordan should move to the third part: "talk to 'em." Which is good, because right now Angela and are just sitting here, staring at each other, then the tablecloth, then our drinks.

I know it's my first time, but I'm pretty sure this isn't how a date is supposed to go. It's a bit like when Angela and I were on the phone and my brain felt empty. Only then I was nervous, but now I feel fine. I just can't come up with anything to talk about. Why not?

An older couple walks by the front window, slowly, and I perk up. Of course! I can't believe I forgot—the whole reason I wanted a table up front was to talk about the people outside!

"Hey," I say to Angela, "check out that couple."

Angela leans toward the window. "What about them?"

"Well, they uh…"

Crap. Why didn't the online review say anything more, like what you're actually supposed to *say* about the people who walk by the front window? I search for something cool, something witty.

"Well, they uh, they look kind of old." Nice one, Chance.

Angela scrunches her eyebrows. "Oh. Yeah, I guess." She stares out the window, first at the street, then up at the sky. Right now, the clouds are more interesting than me. I check the time. I really wish the food would get here. Really.

I chuckle to myself, thinking of how much Zee hates that word.

"What's so funny?" Angela asks.

"Oh … it's just … um … "

Thankfully, right then Jordan and Zee get back to the table, whispering. They both look upset.

"What's going on?" Angela asks.

"Nothing," Jordan says. He shoots me a look. What? What did I do?

Zee crosses her arms. "Oh, that's right, Jordan. Like we've been away this whole time, talking about nothing at all."

"Whatever," Jordan says.

Zee turns to Angela. "What's going on is, we were discussing your new boyfriend Chance here, how *he's* a gentleman, how *he* opens the car door, how *he* doesn't repeat the same jokes over and over, how *he* doesn't make fun of people like Kevin Spielman, how *he* doesn't think it's cool to ignore his date on purpose."

What? New boyfriend? What the heck is Zee doing??

Angela's face turns red.

No no no, this is not going like I planned at all. First we have nothing to talk about, now we're both embarrassed. I need something to save me, something from my list. But I can't remember anything else that's on it. And no way I can just take it out and look at it here.

"I, uh, I need to go to the bathroom too." I push back my chair and head for the sign marked RESTROOMS as fast as I can.

Inside, I take out my list and scan it. The jokes all look like they were written by a second-grader. I've already used the part about kites, and I'm done with all the Home Slice recommendations.

Finally I see the stuff about Memphis and Tennessee. Yes, that's perfect—I can talk to Angela about where she moved from! I fold the list and put in my pocket, then check my hair and face in the mirror. Even if we haven't had much to talk about, at least I still look all right. I adjust my shirt a bit, pick off a stray piece of lint-fluff. Okay, Chance, you can do this. There's still plenty of time. Heck, the food hasn't even come yet.

I smile to myself as I head out of the restroom, thinking about Tennessee trivia. It's called the Volunteer State and some famous people from there are Davy Crockett and, and … I check the list again, real quick. Right—there's also Elvis and Oprah. I tuck the list in my shirt pocket and make my way back to the table.

"Hey," I say, taking a seat. Our pizzas are on the table. Both look awesome.

Zee is chomping on a slice of Pirate's Booty, and there's a crust on her plate. She's already eaten two pieces? Jordan and Angela are talking. I snag a piece of Meatball Moonwalk, the cheese stretching across the table like silly string.

"So that's why you were late to class the first day?" Jordan asks.

Angela nods. "We'd been driving in the whole day before, and my parents overslept."

"That's cool," Jordan says. "We went there once, one summer on vacation."

"Really?"

Zee coughs, too loud, and takes another chunk out of her Pirate's Booty.

"Really," Jordan says, ignoring her. "We drove to Memphis, to Graceland."

"Oooo," Angela says, "that's my favorite part of the state! I love Elvis!"

Hey, wait, what's going on? They can't be talking about Tennessee—that's *my* topic!

"Yeah," Jordan says, "Elvis rocks."

"Where else did you go?" Angela asks.

"Davy Crockett!" I blurt out.

Everyone stares at me. I feel a piece of cheese dangling from my lip.

"Davy Crockett," I repeat, not quite as loud. I wipe the cheese off my mouth. "He, uh, he's from Tennessee."

Zee gives me a little laugh.

"Thanks for the newsflash," Jordan says. "Did

Kevin tell you that, too?"

Kevin? Why does Jordan keep bringing him up? "No," I say, "he didn't tell me anything." And then, before I can stop myself, I add: "Just like you."

Jordan cocks his head. "Like me?"

"Yeah." My voice is barely a whisper.

Jordan tilts back in his chair. Which makes it seem like he's looking down on me, even more than normal. "What's that supposed to mean?" he asks.

Angela and Zee are both staring at me.

"I just … you … you didn't tell me …"

I look down at the tablecloth. It's got a pattern of little red flowers, on a black background.

Jordan lets out a snort. "I'm supposed to tell you stuff, but you can't even tell *me* what it is?" He pauses. "Cole was right. You really are like that Spielman dweeb."

The red flowers start to blur together. He and Cole were talking about me? I picture the two of them joking at football practice, whispering on the bus, playing video games together.

Suddenly the words spew out, like a cut that keeps bleeding no matter how hard I press down to make it stop:

"You didn't tell me about football-camp or you-and-Zee … or your-new-clothes-and-tie-and-cologne … or you-and-Cole or you-two-and-that-stupid-video-game, or …or … anything!"

I'm gripping the edge of the tablecloth so hard my fingers hurt. I've pulled all the plates and cups a couple inches toward me.

What did I just do? I've wanted to say all that to Jordan, ever since the first day of school. But I never pictured myself actually doing it, not out loud. In fact, since we've known each other, I've never really said *anything* to Jordan when he does stuff that bothers me.

I let go of the tablecloth and look up.

Jordan's eyes are wide, his eyebrows close together, like he's surprised and mad at the same time. Then he leans forward, his front chair legs thudding on the floor.

"Dude," Jordan says. "We're in seventh grade now. I can't help it if you can't keep up."

Zee sets her pizza slice on her plate. "Jordan," she says. "That's rude."

Quick as a flash, Jordan reaches over yanks the

list from my shirt pocket.

"Hey!" I yell.

Jordan ignores me. "You think I'm rude?" He tosses the list on the table. "How about making a list of every little thing to say on a date? How about faking your entire conversation, just to impress a girl?"

My face suddenly feels red hot. Jordan's always known about my lists, but he's never—

"What are you talking about?" Angela asks.

"Why don't you ask Chance?" Jordan taps the list. "Or better yet, ask him why he's *always* making lists of what to do, ask him what this list right here is, why he was looking at it when he walked out of the bathroom..."

Sweat beads on my head. And then I feel a pinch in my eye. Oh no, please. Please don't let me start crying, not here, not now.

Zee stands. "I'm ready to go." She grabs her purse. "And Jordan? You're. A. Complete. Ass."

Angela picks up the list, slowly unfolds it. I know there are a ton of other people in the restaurant, talking and laughing, but right now the world's completely silent as she reads.

All of it.

"I … I'm sorry," I say.

Angela folds the list and puts it on the table. "I think I'm ready to go now, too."

Return Call

Mom's in the living room when I get home, watching TV.

"How was your date?"

I muster all that's left of my fakeness, try to give her a smile. My face feels like a rubber band, stretched so thin it's about to break.

"Pretty good," I lie. "But I … I think I'm gonna go lie down. Dating wears me out."

Mom grins. "Of course. I'm glad you had a good time, Chance. You can tell me all about it later."

Or never.

I trudge to my room, close the door, and collapse on my bed.

Your date just imploded and you fought with your best friend. Do you:

Call Angela and apologize? *(Turn to p. 43)*

I lay on my back and toss the baseball up, halfway

to the ceiling. Even if I called Angela right now, she'd probably think I was using a new list, to explain the other one.

Call Jordan and apologize? (Turn to p. 18)

The baseball grazes the ceiling this time, sending a couple flecks of white dust fluttering down. I still can't believe I said all that to Jordan. Or what he did to me.

Live in your closet forever and get home-schooled? (Turn to p. 22)

I catch the baseball and flip it to my throwing hand. By Monday, the whole school will know what happened. If they don't already.

Run away to a new town? I hear Michigan is nice. (Turn to p. 71)

Actually, I bet half of Texas already knows. That's probably my only real option. To move as far away as possible. To a whole different state.

Of course. A different state.

It takes me a couple seconds to fish the slip of paper from my wallet. I unfold it, take out my phone, and dial.

The phone rings three times before it goes to

voicemail.

"Hi-ya! You've reached Jim's cell phone! If you leave a message after the beep, I'll be sure and ring you back as soon as humanly possible!"

I hear Dad's smoker-cough at the very end of the message, then a long beep.

"Hey Dad," I say, "it's me, Chance. Um…" Where do I start? With Jordan? With Angela?

The phone beeps again, and a mechanical voice comes on: "We did not get your message. Press 1 to try again, or 2 to hang up."

Crap. I hit "1" and wait for the long beep.

"Hey, Dad. So, I wanted to talk to you about some stuff. I was … so football is going really good, and…" Why the heck am I talking to him about football? "And anyway, I went on a date but it wasn't … I was thinking maybe I could come out there for Christmas, or maybe sooner if—"

The phone beeps, cutting me off: "We did not get your message. Press 1 to try again, or 2 to hang up."

I stare at the phone, like there's something wrong with it. Then I hang up and flop back onto my bed. I grab the baseball from the floor. But I fall asleep before I can even toss it up once.

*   *   *

The next day, Sunday, is a blur. I tell Mom I'm
not feeling well, stay in my room and in bed the whole
day. I wonder if I can do this for next week. And month.
And year.

I think about calling Dad back again, then realize
he'll see my number on his caller ID, even if my message
didn't go through. So he'll probably call me back,
sometime later.

He doesn't.

Likes

"*Peters!* Get your head in the game!"

Head Coach has been riding me the entire practice. It's like I can't do anything right.

This morning, Jordan and Angela completely ignored me, and Zee's been absent all day. In first period, I almost said something to Jordan, either to apologize or ask how the rest of his weekend was, but it never seemed like the right time. I sent Angela a text over the weekend, just a short one asking what was up, but she never replied. But then, after English, she came up to my locker:

"Chance?"

"Oh, hey Angela. Hi."

"Chance, I think we need to break up."

My throat felt like I swallowed a rock. "I…"

"Not like we were even going together," Angela continued, "but you know what I mean."

164

The rock grew to a boulder. I couldn't speak.

"Anyway," Angela said, "I've got to go to math class. I … I'll see you."

And with that, she walked off. All day long, I've run the scene over and over in my head, probably fifty thousand times.

"Run it again!" Head Coach bellows, jolting me back to the present, to the football field. "And Peters, go up the *middle* this time!"

I trot back to the huddle. We run the same play and I get the handoff, see an opening to the left, but force myself not to go there, instead heading into the thicket of guys in the center. I slam into the back of one of my own linemen, trip over his cleats and fall to the ground. A pile of much bigger guys, like fifty-ton dominoes, collapse on top of me.

Head Coach blows his whistle. "Okay," I hear him say from the bottom of the pile. "At least you hit the right hole, Peters. Next time, try not to get tackled by your own man."

As I wait for the tangle of guys to work their way off me, I try not to replay the Angela conversation in my head. I need a new topic. I think about baseball, how it's nothing like this, how there are no pileups like a highway accident on every play. In baseball, you use skill, not just brute force. I miss baseball.

And then, just like that, squished at the bottom of the pile, it dawns on me.

It's not just that I miss baseball—I'm pretty sure I don't *like* football. I immediately feel guilty, and I can almost hear Dad's words in my head: "You don't *what*?"

What's wrong with me? Am I wimp, just too afraid of getting hit, getting tackled? No, it's not that. I mean, I'm not in love with getting hit, but it's not like I hate it, either. Plus if I really try, I'm pretty darn good at being a running back.

For whatever reason, it makes me think of what Zee said about ice cream—how some people like chocolate, but others pick vanilla. There's no reason why, no right or wrong, no good or bad, it just *is*.

And that's what I feel like right now: My sports taste buds just don't like football.

Well that sucks.

"All right," Head Coach says. "Line it back up! And, Peters?" He doesn't wait for me to answer. "This time, the play is set for the middle. But. If you happen to see a hole somewhere else, *now* you can take it. Now, I want you to go wherever everyone isn't."

Ah-ha, maybe *this* will make me like football. Maybe I just didn't like Head Coach telling me what to do all the time—but now, I can do what I want.

We run the play and I get the ball, head to the center, then see a flash of daylight to the right and burst toward it. A guy grabs my jersey but I break free, sprinting to the end zone. Which should make me ecstatic, thrilled, happy as the first guy in outer space. Instead I feel like a warm bag of monkey poop.

Angela broke up with me. Jordan hates me. And I still don't like football.

But of course I keep that to myself. I try not to even think it too loud. If Head Coach or any of the guys knew I wasn't 100% football, 100% of the time, I'd be an outcast, a leper, an alien from another planet with purple mucous-y skin and seventeen arms and a nose on my elbow and a bucket for a head.

After practice, we're in the locker room and Jordan and Cole are joking about whether Head Coach wears his sunglasses when he sleeps. Neither of them said a word to me, all practice.

As I take off my cleats, I look at the empty locker beside me. I finish with my cleats and take the thigh pad out of my uniform. The top side has the logo on it. Okay. Logo side up, I keep playing football. Logo side down, I don't. I toss the pad and it spins, end-over-end, landing on the floor with a soft plop.

There's no logo showing.

Crap.

There is no way I can quit football. Just the thought of it makes me sick to my stomach. What would I do instead? I would take regular P.E., like Kevin. Like lots of guys, really. And I would practice baseball, practice track, practice the sports I actually like.

But then I think about what everyone would say. I picture Head Coach looking down at me with his shades, slowly shaking his head. No one on the team would ever talk to me again. And the whole school would think I'm a quitter—no way I'd ever get a girlfriend after that. And Dad? He'd probably never call me again.

Okay, I'm sticking with football, like it or not.

Suddenly Cole and Jordan crash through the double-doors, pulling someone behind them.

"Well," Cole says. "Look who we found in the hall."

It's Kevin.

Team Sport, Take Two

They drag Kevin to the center of the locker room.

"I was only in the hall," he says. "I have to get to the P.E. lockers to—"

"I don't care," Cole interrupts. "Remember what I told you? I do. I told you that, if you ever came *near* this locker room again, you were dead."

Kevin looks up at him, then at me. I turn away.

"Hey Jordan," Cole says. "Remember what we learned in football camp? About what happens to quitters?"

Jordan looks confused.

"Give me your shoulder pads," Cole tells him.

Jordan picks up his pads. "They're way too big for … oh." Jordan hesitates. "Do you really think we should?"

"He quit the team," Cole says. "He made us run laps. You think people can just do whatever they want, with no consequences?"

Jordan looks over at me.

Come on, I think, tell Cole to shove it! Jordan's the only guy bigger than Cole, the only guy he would listen to. I concentrate, staring at him, trying to tell Jordan all of that with just my eyes. I think about how Jordan saved me from those high school guys, back when we first became friends. True, Jordan's been a complete jerk lately, but I know him, I've known Jordan Vargas for over two years. He's my best friend. He's the kind of guy who helps people.

But then Jordan looks at Cole, at the rest of the locker room, and his shoulders sag a little. He hands his pads to Cole.

What the?

Cole grins, puts the pads over Kevin's head, straps them in place. The whole time Kevin just sits there, looking bewildered.

Why doesn't Kevin try to get away? What's Cole going to do?

Cole pulls Kevin across the floor toward the showers. Now Kevin struggles, dragging his feet and trying to twist away from Cole's grip, but it doesn't do any good. Even with the shoulder pads, Cole is twice his size. I want to tell Cole to leave him alone, but I just stand there.

"Hold him down," Cole tells Jordan.

Jordan does what he says, while Cole strips off Kevin's pants. Kevin is now wearing just his underwear and shoulder pads. He looks terrified.

"I don't like football," Kevin says, his voice tiny. "What's wrong with that?"

Cole barks out a laugh. *"I don't like football,"* he mocks. "Football, Spielman, is a team sport. It doesn't matter whether you *like* it."

Together, he and Jordan stand Kevin up, then push him against the shower wall. A bunch of wet towels hang there on hooks. Cole throws the towels to the floor and then they lift Kevin, hooking his shoulder pads. When they let go he hangs there, halfway up the wall, legs dangling.

"Perfect!" Cole says.

I look around. A few guys are laughing, but most are quiet. Everyone is staring at Kevin. Maybe I can sneak out, get Head Coach.

But Cole walks over to the double-doors. He looks out the window, checks the hall. "Okay," he says. "Jordan. Ball."

Jordan tosses him a football.

"Now," Cole says, "time for a little game. It's called Pin the Ball on the Quitter. Everyone gets a shot. But I'll go first."

Cole holds the football toward Kevin and squints, like he's scoping a target. "You get a point if you hit the head." He rears back. "Or if you hit the *groin.*" On the last word he fires the football across the room. It spirals at Kevin, slamming into his exposed thigh.

Kevin lets out a whimper.

"Well damn," Cole says. "Just missed."

There's a bright red mark on Kevin's leg, where the football hit.

"Not like he'd feel it anyway," Jordan says. "You gotta have *balls* to play football!"

A few guys crack up at this.

Jordan and Cole fist-bump. "Nice!" Cole says. "I forgot about that part!"

That part?

Is "that part" something else he learned from Cole, or at football camp? It sure doesn't sound like anything Jordan would say. At least, not the Jordan I know. Or used to know.

"Okay," Cole says, tossing Jordan the ball. "You're up."

Jordan catches the ball and stands there, halfway across the room. It reminds me a little of last summer, when we were at the *Guess Your Speed!* game booth.

There is no way he'll do this. It's one thing for him to give Cole his pads, help him hold Kevin down. But no way he would throw a football at Kevin Spielman, at someone just hanging on a wall. He's not like Cole, he's—

Jordan fires the ball across the room. It bounces off the wall, hard, beside Kevin's head.

No.

"Aww, so close!" Cole says. He picks up the ball. "Okay, who else?"

The other guys are standing at their lockers, some laughing and smiling, but nobody steps forward.

"Come on," Cole says. "No one wants a shot at the quitter?"

A few guys whisper to each other.

"Well," Cole says, "while you girls are making up your minds, I'll go again. And this time, I won't miss."

He smiles a wicked grin. "Footballllll," Cole's

voice is deep, imitating Head Coach, "is all about *collision*." He holds the ball up and shuffles back and forth, like he's looking for a receiver.

On the wall, Kevin's eyes are wide behind his glasses. A tear streams down his cheek. The mark on his thigh is darker, turning purplish. He tries to cross his legs to protect himself, but keeps slipping against the wall. If Cole hits him again…

I grab my cleat and hurl it as hard as I can, like I'm throwing out a runner all the way from the outfield. The cleat blurs through the air, whipping end-over-end toward Cole. But it veers off and hits Jordan, slamming into his nose and eye with a sharp crack.

"Dude!" Jordan yells. "What the hell?"

I'm wondering the same thing.

Jordan touches his eye and winces; there's a red spot underneath it.

"*Dude.*" He says it again, this time not as loud, but angrier. The spot turns darker, reddish-blue. A trickle of blood seeps from his nose.

Oh crap crap crap. What am I doing sticking up for Kevin Spielman? I never stick up for anyone. Much less the guy who quit football, the guy who's probably the biggest loser in the entire school.

Cole glares at me. "What's your problem, *Peters*?" He lowers the football. "Just because you're one of our best players, don't think I won't hang your ass right there next to the Quitter."

All the guys are looking at me. Will Cole really hang me on the wall like he did to Kevin?

Will Jordan help him?

Truth

"Tell me," Cole says.

I have no idea what he's talking about.

"Tell me why," Cole says, jabbing a finger in Kevin's rib. "Why you stuck up for this Quitter. Why you chunked a cleat at your best friend's face. Are you and the Quitter all buddy-buddy now?"

For a split-second I think about doing a half-laugh, of saying that yes, that's *exactly* why I did it, and then I'll pretend it was all a big joke.

But instead I look at Jordan. His nose is dripping blood, eye swollen shut. What happened? Last year, we hung out all the time. Then he went to football camp, and started hanging out with Cole, and now's he more … he's more … what?

I turn away from Cole, walk to Jordan. It's hard to tell what he's thinking—even more than normal—with his face so messed up. I'm close enough now that he could take a swipe at me if he wanted. And I know how hard he can hit. I also know that Cole, and everyone else, is watching.

I flinch as Jordan raises his hand. He pauses, wipes blood from his face.

"I … I'm sorry about the cleat," I say. "I was aiming for *him*." I point behind Jordan.

He turns, follows my finger. Then he laughs.

"I knew you were still a gamer, Chance-man." Jordan's voice is thick and nasally.

For a moment I'm not sure what he's talking about. Then I realize he thinks I'm pointing at Kevin, still hanging on the wall.

Cole laughs, too. "Damn, Peters, you had me worried for a second!" He steps away from Kevin and walks over to the cleat, picking it up. My hand shakes— my whole arm does—as I follow Cole, keeping my finger pointed straight at him.

Cole stops. His mouth hangs open in disbelief.

The locker room goes completely, absolutely quiet.

Jordan steps closer, right in my face.

I lower my arm. It's still shaking.

What am I supposed to do? What am I supposed to say? I wish I had a list for this. "What To Do When

Your Friendship Goes to Crap." What would be on it? And would it help?

"I don't hate you," I say to Jordan. "I just…"

What? Why *did* I throw the cleat?

Was I sticking up for Kevin? Maybe. But I was also sticking up for me.

Suddenly I know. I know what I should do—what I need to do. The words are in my head, but stuck.

If I say them, what will everyone think? And can I handle it?

Jordan blinks his one good eye at me, waiting. It's almost like he's asking me himself:

Can you handle it?

When I walk down the halls, will everyone laugh and point, or worse?

Can you handle it?

I don't know if I can. But one thing I do know: I can't keep doing things I don't like, just because everyone else does. Like Zee said, maybe it's time to take a chance.

"I just…"

I clear my throat, say the words to Jordan, but loud enough for everyone to hear.

"I don't hate you. I just don't like … I don't like football."

For once, I think I can read Jordan. I'm pretty sure he knows I'm not just talking about football.

Consequences

Slowly, Jordan shakes his head at me.

"This," Cole says, "is completely stupid. Let's just—"

"Shut it."

The words come from Jordan. And, for once, Cole shuts up.

Jordan is still staring at me. I can't tell if he's going to hit me, stick me on the wall next to Kevin, or worse. My legs feel weak. I want to leave. Want to run out and get Head Coach and tell him what happened and let him sort it all out, let him make Cole and Jordan run fifty thousand laps, tell me that it's okay if I don't like football. But I stay put.

"I don't get you," Jordan finally says.

You never really have, I think to myself. All the time we've been friends, I've liked my CYOA books, space stuff, baseball. And Jordan…

"You … you love football," I say.

"Of course," Jordan says.

I search for the right words. "And I think …
we're just … different."

"No kidding," Cole sneers.

Jordan keeps his eyes on me. For a second, he
seems kind of sad. Or maybe I just want him to be.

"Whatever," Jordan says. "It doesn't matter."

"Exactly," I say.

I'm about to tell him it's like how some people
like chocolate better than vanilla, and he's a chocolate
person, I'm more vanilla. But that doesn't *matter*,
neither's right or wrong, good or bad—

"Just *leave*," Jordan says. His voice is harsh.

And suddenly I feel deflated, like a kite falling to
the ground. Now, I know for sure.

Things have changed.

From the corner of my eye, I see Cole nodding. I
know that, if I looked over at him, he'd be wearing a big
stupid grin.

But instead I turn to Kevin, still hanging from the
wall. Before I can think about it, I walk over and unhook
him. Kevin drops to the floor, then stands. I hand him
his pants and he puts them on.

"Hey…" Cole says.

I stand there, next to Kevin, waiting. Can I handle it?

"Whatever," Jordan says. "It doesn't matter. Go hang with your new best friend, Chance. And don't show up here again, don't talk to me in school, don't call me, don't anything. We're done."

My legs are shaking and I feel like I could puke. But I don't. I turn and walk out the double-doors with Kevin. No one tries to stop us.

Head Coach

Kevin is silent as we walk down the hall.

"Spielman!"

Head Coach's voice freezes us.

"Where're you going, with those pads?"

I totally forgot—Kevin is still wearing Jordan's

shoulder pads.

"I, uh…"

Kevin quickly takes off the oversized pads.

"That's school property," Head Coach says. He's

standing over us, sunglasses reflecting down. "And

Peters, why are you letting Spielman wear your pads?

He's not on the team anymore, remember?"

"Those aren't…"

How can I tell him those are Jordan's pads? If I

do, I'll have to explain what happened, what Cole and

Jordan did to Kevin. It's one thing to tell Jordan how I

feel about football. It's totally different to rat him out.

I glance at Kevin. He's just standing there, like

he's in a daze.

"It's up to you," I say to him. If he wants to tell on Cole and Jordan, I'm totally behind him. But I know that's got to be his call.

"Peters," Head Coach says, "what the Sam Hill are you talking about?"

I stare at Kevin, trying to tell him without speaking that, whatever he decides, I'll back him up. I hope he can read me better than Jordan. He looks pale and his eyes are wide, like he's somewhere else, maybe still back in the locker room. But then, he meets my gaze, seems to understand. He hands the pads to me.

"I'm sorry," Kevin tells Head Coach. "I just wanted to see what it felt like to wear them, one last time." Kevin nods at me, his eyes not so wide anymore. "Chance was telling me to put them back, when you stopped us."

"I thought you didn't like football, Spielman. Are you changing your mind?"

"No, sir. I just—just wanted to be sure."

Head Coach shakes his head. "Sometimes, I just don't understand you kids." He turns to me. "Peters, go put those pads back in the locker room. And don't let me ever catch you loaning school property out like that again." He heads down the hall to his office.

I stand there, holding the pads.

"Wait," I say.

Head Coach stops. "What is it, Peters?"

"I … I've got something to tell you."

I walk up to Head Coach, and hand him the pads.

"What are you doing, Peters?"

I stand there, looking up at the huge man, hidden behind his sunglasses. This guy loves football even more than Jordan. Maybe even more than Dad. What will he think of me?

"I…"

Suddenly Kevin is at my side. Somehow, that makes it easier.

"I don't really want to be on the team anymore, sir."

"I don't have time for jokes, Pe—"

"I'm not joking, sir."

Head Coach tilts his head. "But Peters, you're one of my best players. And you can take a hit like the best of them, and keep going."

My legs are shaking again. "I—thank you, sir. But I … I just don't think I'm a football person. It's just

186

not me."

Head Coach is silent. I swallow a lump from my throat.

"I'm sorry, sir."

And then Head Coach does the last thing I expect. He takes off his sunglasses.

I'm not sure what I thought his eyes would look like. Maybe hard bits of black, or ice cold blue, or even burnt orange like our school colors. But they're not—they're green. And super-light, like lime sherbet. They're surrounded by a bunch of wrinkles at the corners, like he laughs. A lot.

"What in the world are you sorry for, Peters?"

"I … because I don't like football, sir."

A smile flashes across Head Coach's face, just like he did when Kevin quit.

"Peters. You can't help what you *like*. Hell, that's what makes life life."

"You're not mad?"

Head Coach laughs. Actually, really, laughs. "Peters, you're fast, you can take a hit. Some people quit because they're scared, or think they're not good enough. *Those* people I get mad at. But not liking the game?

Hell, that's the best reason there is not to play. No sense in doing what you hate, if you don't have to."

He takes the pads. "And I'm not an idiot—to walk away from football, at your age, in this state? That takes some serious ballsack."

Head Coach puts his sunglasses on. "No, Peters, I'm not mad." He nods at Kevin. "At either of you."

"Thank you, sir." We both say it at once.

"And boys?"

"Yes, sir?"

"Please don't tell anyone I said ballsack."

Taste Buds

The next day on the bus, Jordan is sitting halfway back, beside Cole. Neither of them looks up when I get on. They're still ignoring me. And now, so are a bunch of other guys.

I get that sick, sort of empty feeling in my stomach. Can I really handle this? Can I handle Jordan and half the guys pretending I don't exist? I could go tell him I'm sorry, I was just being stupid, I want everything the way it used to be.

But do I want that? Really?

I picture Zee giving me her look for saying "Really." She's back today, sitting a few rows behind Jordan with another girl. She smiles and gives me a quick wave.

So, at least not everyone's ignoring me. And she and Jordan aren't sitting together—I wonder if they broke up.

I wave back then take a seat, in the very front row. Kevin scoots over to make room. He's wearing jeans, a plain blue T-shirt, and sneakers. For the first time, he's dressed like—well, like everyone else.

"What?" he asks, looking down at himself. "Do I still have donut on my shirt?"

I shake my head. "No, you just usually wear something more, I don't know…"

"Crazy?" Kevin says.

"Yeah. Kinda."

"I have to admit," he says, "this is one of my least favorite outfits. But today's laundry day, so I didn't have much to choose from. Plus, I do have *some* regular clothes. I'm not as dumb as I look, you know."

"Well…"

"Hey," Kevin says, "you're supposed to agree with me on that."

"Oh yeah. Right." I try to sound sarcastic, but I'm not sure if he gets it.

Kevin opens his backpack and takes out a small package, wrapped in newspaper comics. It's shaped like a book, but lumpy on top. "I wanted to tell you thanks," he says. "For helping me yesterday."

His hands are trembling a bit as he hands it over. I'm about to ask what's wrong, then I realize how stupid that is. Yesterday he was hanging on a wall, half-naked, with guys beaming a football at him. He still hasn't told anyone about it. If I'd been through the same thing, I'd probably have more than just jittery hands. I probably wouldn't even be at school.

"Thanks," I say.

Kevin smiles. "You know, people usually say thanks *after* they open gifts."

"Yeah, it's just…" I don't tell him it's the first gift I've ever gotten outside my birthday or Christmas.

I rip off the newspaper. Inside is a worn CYOA book: *Lost Civilization of the Tundra.* On top of it is a round, black rock.

"Do you have that book?" Kevin asks.

"No."

"Cool. But, I checked it out from the public library. So, technically, you can only keep it for two weeks."

"You gave me a library book as a gift?"

"Uh-huh."

"That's pretty funny."

"I thought so, too."

"A library book and a rock?"

"Oh, that's not just a rock. It's a *moon* rock."

"This—it's actually from the moon?"

"Sure," Kevin says. "Well, at least, it *could* be. I found it in our backyard."

A fake moon rock and a checked-out library book.

"Thanks," I say. "Again."

"Sure."

Kevin closes his backpack. "So, what are you gonna do?" he asks.

"About what?"

"About what happened with Angela."

"You know about that?"

"Everybody does."

"Oh."

I wonder if she told the whole school, or if Jordan did. I guess it doesn't really matter.

"I'm not sure," I say.

I think back to Home Slice, how Angela and I really didn't have anything to talk about, even with my lists.

"I think Angela and I are just different, you know?" I pause. "The same as with me and Jordan…"

Kevin nods. "Kind of like how we all have

different taste buds, so some people like chocolate, and others like vanilla?"

"I can't believe you just said that."

"Why?"

"It's—well, I was thinking the exact same thing."

"That happens sometimes. Actually, I read that the odds for it happening are really good, the longer two people know each other."

"Yeah, maybe… Anyway, I think that's exactly right. Jordan's more of a chocolate person."

"And you're more vanilla?"

I think about Angela and her vanilla shampoo.

"I like vanilla," I say, "but it's not my favorite."

*   *   *

At school, I notice my locker from halfway down the hall. There's something written on it. As I get closer, I see the message, in big black letters:

QUITTER.

A few kids are looking at it, laughing. Others are shaking their heads. I can't tell if they're doing that at me, or at whoever wrote on my locker.

"I already called the janitor," says a deep voice from behind.

I turn and see Head Coach.

"Might have to paint over it," he says, "which could take a couple days."

"Oh," I say. I picture my locker becoming the main attraction for the week.

"Chance," Head Coach says, "can I give you two pieces of advice?" His low and rumbly voice shakes the middle of my chest.

"Um, sure."

Like I'm going to say no.

"First thing is, you can't scratch every itch. Life's all about making choices."

I'm not exactly sure what he's talking about. "Uh-huh," I say, nodding.

"And second, think about trying out for baseball, in the spring."

"What?"

"I already know you're fast. Word is, you've got a decent arm, too."

How does he know about my arm, that I even play baseball?

"Football's not the only thing I coach," he says. He gives me a quick nod, then walks off.

194

*   *   *

In first period, Angela is not at her desk. Instead, someone else is sitting there. A guy I barely know, Greg Metzer. I scan the room and see Angela, sitting near the back corner. She and Greg must have switched desks. I can only imagine what Angela told Ms. Fernandez to make that happen. Great.

Jordan is still sitting behind me. He looks up when I walk to my desk, but doesn't say a word. I wonder if he had anything to do with the graffiti.

After class, QUITTER is still on my locker. It's a little faded, where the janitor tried to wash it off, but it must be in permanent marker. They'll definitely have to paint over it.

As I turn the combination, Zee walks up.

"Hey, Chance." She puts her huge backpack, roughly the size of Jupiter, on the floor.

"Hey," I say.

"Sorry about Saturday. Jordan's just…" She sighs. "We broke up."

"Oh."

Zee's wearing a bright red shirt—the same one from our Home Slice double date.

"Anyway," she says, "I just … I'm not mad at you or anything, right? I still like you."

I feel all the blood rush to my face. It's probably the exact same color as her shirt.

"Uh, yeah," I stammer. "Okay."

Zee hefts her gargantuan backpack over a shoulder.

"All right," she says, "see ya later."

As she walks off, hunched over from her backpack, I think again about Jordan being more of a chocolate person, Angela being vanilla. I look at Zee's shirt. Maybe I'm more of a strawberry person.

"Hey, Zee!" I cry out. A bunch of heads turn in the hall. What am I doing?

Zee stops and looks back.

"Um … thanks!" I yell at her. And, for some stupid reason, wave.

Zee tilts her head, then grins and waves back.

Her wave is a bit sideways and off-balance, from trying to hold her super-heavy pack and shooting her hand up in the air at the same time. Not an easy thing to do, I think to myself.

I bet she's got a great throwing arm.

*   *   *

The rest of the day goes by like normal. That is, aside from most of the football guys ignoring me. I wonder if this is how it's going to be, for the rest of the year. For the rest of my life. I could still go back, re-join the team, no problem.

But would it really be no problem? Would everyone just forget what happened, what I said? Would I?

In sixth period, I head to sports but walk past the huge double-doors. At the end of the hall, I push open the smaller, single door to the P.E. locker room. It's exactly like it was last year—a few of the light bulbs out, a few others buzzing like they're on their last legs (or filaments or whatever it is for light bulbs), the concrete floor chipped and cracked in a bunch of places, wire mesh locker-baskets lining most of the walls.

A group of guys are changing into shorts and sneakers. These are the guys who don't play football— I'm surprised how many there are.

"Chance!"

I see Kevin, sitting on a bench across the room, motioning to me. I walk over.

"The locker next to mine's empty," Kevin says. "You can take it if you want."

I pull out the metal basket, drop my gym bag in it. "Just like in football," I say.

Kevin pauses for a second.

That was so, so dumb of me. He's probably still freaked out about what happened, and here I am bringing it up again.

"I'm sorry," I say.

"It's fine," Kevin says. He motions to the room. "At least they don't have shower hooks in here," he says, and smiles a little.

"Or cleats," I say.

He gives me a quick laugh. "You really did nail him."

"Yeah," I say.

I'm still not sure if that was the right thing. But, like Dad used to say, "You can't change the past." Funny to think of him, right now. I can't imagine how Dad would take it, if he knew I was in the P.E. locker room instead of playing football. Would he ignore me, the same as Cole and Jordan and the other football guys? I have the sudden urge to grab my bag and leave, head to the huge double-doors down the hall.

But I don't. Dad has no idea I quit football. Because he never called me back.

And because he's not even *here*, I tell myself. Dad's wanted me to play football since forever. But, if he's not around, why should I fake it?

I try to imagine Dad's reaction, when he does find out. Will he treat me the same way Cole and Jordan have? As I sit there, thinking about the last time I talked to him, really truly talked to him, I realize the truth: Will he treat me the same way Cole and Jordan have?

He already has.

"Are you okay?"

Kevin is staring at me. I've been tying and re-tying the same shoelace on my sneaker. It's bone-tight around my ankle. I loosen the knot.

"Yeah," I say. "I was just … I wish I had a football."

"A football? What for?"

"So I could chunk it in the trash," I say.

"I don't think Head Coach would be too happy about that," Kevin says.

I look at him. He's grinning a bit.

"Yeah," I say. "Maybe I'll wait 'til I get home."

"Good idea," Kevin says.

He leans down to tie his sneakers. The laces are bright red on one, black on the other. He finishes, then sits up.

"So," Kevin says, "I was wondering…"

"Yeah?"

"My parents, they've been bugging me…"

"You're wondering about *that*? Don't even get me started about my dad."

Kevin laughs. "No, no—they've been bugging me about having someone over. They even bought this new video game, and, well…"

He trails off again. He's trying to invite me to come over to his house. I think about how I said no to him about Space Club last week. And I realize how much guts it takes, to ask me to do something with him again.

"That sounds cool," I say.

"Yeah?"

"Yeah. But, one thing."

Kevin's face falls a bit. "What?"

I think back, to how Jordan used to have me over to his house, to play video games or football, but how he

never came to my place. How I never really asked him
to.

"How about you come over to my house," I say.

CYOA, Take Two

The next weekend, Kevin brings his new game system over and Mom helps us hook it to the TV. She's surprisingly good at getting it set up. And she makes us grilled cheese, joking with Kevin about how the cheese in Texas is better than Vermont.

Sometimes, every once in a while, Mom can actually be cool. I just hope she doesn't break out the toothpicks.

She doesn't—instead, after dinner, she brings out ice cream. It's Neapolitan—chocolate, vanilla and strawberry, all mixed together.

"This flavor is my favorite," Kevin says, "but my parents hardly ever buy it. They're not big on sweets." He spoons a huge bite into his mouth. He's got ice cream smeared on one cheek.

I remember something he said, back on the bus.

"Do your parents really go out to the lake, and just skip rocks?" I ask.

"Of course," Kevin says. "Best way to get to know someone."

Mom rests her chin on her hands. "Your dad and I did that once," she says. "He drove me to the coast for a date, and we just stood there, talking and throwing rocks into the ocean. It was ... nice."

We sit there, eating our ice cream in silence.

I wonder what Mom is thinking about. Dad? Skipping rocks? And I wonder what Kevin's thinking about, too. What happened in football? Space Club? His parents?

I remember back to earlier in the week, when Zee waved at me in the hall. I bet she could skip a mean rock.

For a second, I want to take out a piece of paper and start a new List. But I don't. Some things I don't need to write down. Not anymore.

It's weird how much things have changed—with football, with Angela, with Jordan, with the way half the guys at school won't talk to me. A lot of things suck right now.

But other stuff has changed, too. Stuff that's not so bad.

There's Zee, for one. Will she and I go out? Who

knows.

And there's Kevin. Will he and I be good friends?
Who knows.

(I kind of hope so, for both.)

It makes me think about what Head Coach said,
that life's all about making choices. Lately I've made
some pretty crappy, dead-end ones. But maybe that's
changing.

*You're sitting at the table, eating ice cream with
Mom and Kevin. Do you:*

*Call Dad—no, send him a letter—telling
him you quit football? (Turn to p. 50)*

Text Zee, just to say Hi? (Turn to p. 200)

*Ask Kevin about the next Space Club
meeting? (Turn to p. 73)*

*Tell Mom to please, put away the floss?
(Turn to p. 4)*

www.ingramcontent.com/pod-product-compliance
Lightning Source LLC
Chambersburg PA
CBHW031600310726
48974CB00003B/752